FIGHTING
FELIX
War Angels MC

Table of Contents

Prologue
Lix
Jordan

"Hey Major, maybe we should let the newbie drive!" Corporal Riggs called to our commanding officer from the back of the Humvee we were all stuck in. I was the newbie, this was my first tour ever and like any newbie I was determined to make a good impression.

"Does Private Taggart know where we're going?" The Major called back.

"No sir I do not but if you have a map I can figure it out!" I replied and we all chuckled. Maps were hard to come by around here and we all knew it.

"No worries Private we've got it –"before the Major could finish his sentence the world around us exploded and the Humvee flipped and rolled down a shallow embankment.

Along the way I must have slammed my head against something because my vision blurred and my ears started to ring. When we stopped rolling we were stuck buckled into our seats upside down. I could feel wetness dripping into my hair from somewhere on either side of my head but I ignored it.

I didn't feel much pain other than a bit of whiplash, but the ringing was starting to drive me nuts. I put my fingers in my ears to try to clear them and my hands came away wet. I looked at my hands and found them covered in blood.

The IED must have been left over from another ambush because no insurgents jumped out of the bushes to shoot at us. It looked like I was the one injured the worst so we didn't worry about calling a helo to extract us.

We all unbuckled our belts and climbed up the embankment and jumped into one or another of the other two Humvees that were in our convoy and kept going.

The ringing didn't stop long into the night and I was having trouble hearing guys who were sitting right next to me yelling in my ear. I had been checked out by a doctor when we had first gotten to base but they had said the ringing would go away eventually.

From what I could tell it was getting louder and it was making walking a straight line difficult. Finally after midnight when I couldn't sleep from the sound I got up and made my way over to the med tent.

"I don't know what to tell you," the doctor on duty said, shrugging. "Best we can do is get you on a transfer to Landstuhl and get you an MRI and/or CT Scan. We're pretty limited here as to what we can do."

I was having a hard time understanding the doctor. I was trying to read his lips but wasn't getting very far. Finally I made him write everything down.

"Yeah, I figured. I'll talk to my Commander." The doctor winced while I was talking so I figured I must have been yelling, but I couldn't tell since I couldn't hear myself over the ringing.

I ended up in Landstuhl not long after but I wasn't an emergency so I really just hung out in Germany until a chance to get into one of the machines came open. Then I sat in the doctor's office while he told me that I had a TBI, traumatic brain injury, and it had caused my brain to not understand sound or some such. I wasn't actually listening because I couldn't hear him and again I had to get him to write it down. Fuck, was this my life now?

Because of this injury I was sent home and discharged. One tour, one trip in a Humvee and I'm done. I couldn't believe it, seriously messed up.

Ash

I couldn't believe it; I was actually going to meet my sister! Finally, it had only taken seven years to find her and she had actually found me. I was only six months old when my aunt and uncle adopted me but my sister Grace-Lynn is five years older and my aunt didn't want her so she went to foster care. I couldn't believe it when my uncle told me that. I was so mad and I was only ten. Now I was seventeen and she was finally here!

My aunt, who I always thought was my mom, died and my uncle, who was really my dad, promised to find Grace-Lynn. He tried so hard, searched everywhere, paid lawyers exorbitant amounts of money and still nothing.

Then she got involved with the wrong people who did horrible things to her and dumped her on the doorstep of a motorcycle club. It was one of those bikers who found me and set up a meeting for us to meet.

He was bringing her here now and I was standing at the front window watching for his truck to come back. He was huge, he towered over my dad and I. I was close to six feet tall, and dad was just over six feet but this guy was massive.

I wondered if my sister was tall like me, or short like dad said our mom was. I wondered so many things about my sister and now I would get to ask her.

When the truck pulled up again in front of the house, the tall man got out and went around the other side. He stood in the passenger door of the truck for a few minutes talking to whoever sat there, then finally stepped away holding a girl's hand. She stepped out and I felt like I was looking in a mirror. She could have been my twin, even though she was five years older than me.

She was tall and slender like I was and her hair was just as red but cut short and spiky. I couldn't see her eyes but I bet they were gray just like mine and her skin creamy and spattered with freckles. I couldn't wait any longer; I rushed to the front door, whipped it open and launched myself into my sister's arms. I finally had her, best tenth birthday gift ever!

CHAPTER 1

Lix

I looked at the address on the piece of paper I was holding and sighed. I had only been back in Canada for about six months since the Humvee accident. I had spent that time at my parent's house in Kelowna getting used to my new normal, which was a constant ringing in my ears to the point that I couldn't hear anything and learning sign language. I could still speak, but I couldn't whisper and I couldn't hear myself even when I was yelling, which I was doing a lot of apparently.

My parents thought I was wasting away at their house and I needed to get out and live my life. I wasn't sure what that meant since I didn't have a life. I was only 20 and the one thing I wanted to do all my life, serve in the Canadian Armed Forces and serve with JTF 2, was no longer an option. .

So, I spent my time in my bedroom, living off my pension which was tiny, and drawing. Drawing was the only other thing I ever wanted to do with my time.

My oldest sister Bethie had been visiting one day with her four kids and had told me about a group here in Kamloops that was helping vets like me. Only not like me cause those other guys had actually served. I had flown in a plane over to Jordan, sat on base for a week or so, driven in a Humvee and been sent home. That was my illustrious army career.

Either way Bethie had gotten me the information and Lillian, my second sister, had called and talked to Lo. Lillian had three kids and they were all running around crazy at my mother's house. Thank God I couldn't hear anything. As Lillian was talking to Lo my youngest sister Petra showed up with her daughter.

Bethie was older than me by ten years, Lillian older by six years and Petra older by three years. I was the youngest of four and the only boy. I wore doll clothes more often as a baby than I did regular clothes. It was like having four mothers and often my sisters still tried to mother me.

Which was why I was standing here looking up at the front gates of the War Angel's MC gate. The gate itself was wide open to a gravel parking lot with a huge flat building four or so car lengths from the gate. One side of the building looked like a garage of sorts for motorcycle and car repair.

The other side looked like apartments or private rooms and right in the middle was the main door into the clubhouse which really looked like a seedy bar from the outside. Stenciled on the door was a soldier, kneeling with his head bowed and holding dog tags and behind him were ragged and torn angel wings. I got the name before, War Angel's, but now it really made sense.

Making up my mind to just get this over with I stepped into the clubhouse and see what this life was all about. Besides, July in Kamloops is way too hot to be hanging around outside; hopefully these guys had splurged on air conditioning.

As the door closed behind me the first person I saw was a guy an inch or so shorter than me whose arms were covered in tattoos. I could also see tats peeking out the top of his shirt collar. He was not wearing a t-shirt; he was wearing a long sleeved button up shirt with the sleeves rolled up.

Holy fuck, wasn't he hot? He gave me a chin lift as he walked by and left the clubhouse. I looked around but no one else was around. I waited for a few more minutes but no one appeared so I called out.

"Uh, hello, is anyone here?" I looked around again but still no one appeared. I felt like an idiot standing in the middle of an empty room but what the hell was I supposed to do? I called out again, "Hello? I'm here to meet, uh Logan Winters! Is Logan Winters here?"

A big man came storming out of a room on the other side of the main room and his mouth was moving but of course I couldn't hear what he was actually saying.

"Hey buddy, I can't hear you, no matter how loud you yell at me." I shrugged, shaking my head.

"Fuck," the guy swore, tipping his head back and slamming his hands on his hips.

"That I got, I'm not so good at reading lips but that one's pretty easy." I said pointing and smiling.

Sorry, the guy signed, *I'm Logan Winters, call me Lo.*

"Hey, I'm Lix." I said waving a bit. "I can talk, just not hear so feel free to tell me if I'm yelling."

Sure, Lo signed chuckling. *Come into the office and we'll get shit figured out.*

Ashlyn

It was July. I had just graduated from high school. I was working at my dad's dentist office while I decided what I wanted to do with my life. I really had no idea, except that I didn't want anything to do with people's mouths.

I sat at the desk waiting for the phone to ring doodling on a piece of paper when one of the hygienists came up from the back.

"Hey, that's cool Ash!" She said looking over my shoulder at the doodle. "What is that?"

"Nothing really," I said, shrugging. "Just bored and doodling."

"That would make a really cool tattoo. You should post that on Facebook or something and sell designs."

"Huh, would people really want that?"

"Isn't your sister with one of those motorcycle guys? They have a tattoo parlor, you should go in there and ask."

"Really? The War Angels have a tattoo parlor?"

"Yeah, I can't remember who actually owns it, but it's WAMC Tats or something like that."

"I've been thinking about getting a tattoo anyway, I think I'll go over there after work."

I only had an hour left at the office so I had time to talk myself into it. I really had been thinking about getting a tattoo, a pixie actually for my sister since that what her boyfriend called her. I had drawn it a few days after I had first met her and Aiden, her boyfriend kept calling her Pixie.

I could see why he called her that. Even at five foot eleven Grace-Lynn was way shorter than Aiden who was six foot eight, and with her short red hair she kind of looked like a fairy.

I left the office and hopped in my car. I had searched up the tattoo parlor on my phone so I knew where I was going and it was really a short drive.

I turned my music up loud and hit afternoon traffic. Ten minutes later I was parking in front of WAMC Tat's. Crazy, I had never seen it here before.

Walking into the shop was like a breath of fresh air with the air conditioning but the guy behind the counter was what hit me first. He was tall, not as tall as Aiden, but at least six foot three or four and he was super well built.

His t-shirt was tight enough that I could see the muscles defined through the thin cotton and it was a sight to behold. He lifted a hand to push his fingers through his messy black hair that had fallen into his eyes.

I walked up to the counter thinking he was ignoring me since I had heard the bells above the door when I walked in. I stood at the counter for a couple seconds before the guy looked up and jumped like I had scared him. He took a deep breath, holding one hand over his heart like he thought it would burst from his chest and the other out to me.

"You scared me." He yelled at me. My eyes widened unsure what I should say or do at this point. Besides being yelled at his eyes held me captive, they were such a dark brown that they looked black. "Sorry, too loud?"

I nodded, still not sure if I should say anything and then he smiled.

"I'm deaf," he said, his smile widening and I felt my own lips answering the smile. "I didn't hear you come in and then you were right in front of me. What can I do to help you?"

"Do you hire artists?" I asked, smiling as he watched my lips.

"You're looking for an artist?"

"No," I said, shaking my head. "Do you have a pen and paper?" I asked, mimicking writing.

He nodded and looked around then came up with an art pencil and sketch pad. I quickly wrote my question and handed the sketch pad back.

"Oh, I don't know, I've only been working here for a couple of weeks." He said, shrugging. "I can pass this on to the boss though if you want to leave your name and number?"

I nodded and took the sketch pad back and wrote my information on the page, then wrote another question about getting a tattoo.

"We can make an appointment for you if you want." He said, pulling out a giant book.

My eyes must have almost popped out of my head because he stopped and waited for me to do something. I took the pad and pencil again and wrote that I wanted to talk to my sister, Pixie before I did anything but I would get back to them when I knew more.

"Pixie? Is that Seether's girl?" The guy asked looking up at me, his gaze snapping into mine. I nodded feeling strange that I was having a complete conversation with this guy and I hadn't spoken a word in ten minutes. "Seether said he was on his way over to check the cameras if you want to hang out a minute. I'm sure Pixie will be with him."

I suddenly freaked. I didn't know why but I just couldn't stay. I grabbed the pencil and pad and wrote that I would talk to her later and that I had to run but I would be back and then I turned and rushed out of the shop.

Damn I was a fool. What was wrong with me? I was a fool, that's what was wrong with me.

CHAPTER 2

Lix

The girl, Ashlyn sure rushed out of the shop in a hurry. I wondered if it was me but I couldn't think of a reason why. I hadn't done anything scary I didn't think. Ashlyn was super-hot so I was on my best behaviour but maybe I had come on too strong?

Whatever, I talked to Seether when he stopped in later that day to look at the cameras and he just shrugged when I asked him about Ashlyn. He said her sister didn't make any sense either and he had intimate knowledge of her.

Three days later I walked into the shop to find Needles already here. That was normal and I knew the guy well enough to know he didn't do it because he didn't trust his staff. I looked at the appointment book and saw Ashlyn's name there.

"Hey, what's on the schedule for the day?" I asked looking down at the appointment book. I know Needles would talk to me unless I was looking at him so I read over the appointments before I looked back up. "Says here Ashlyn Cameron? Is that Pixie's sister?"

"I think so." He said, shrugging.

"Huh, it says here it's just a consult," I said looking down at the book again. Everyone thought I forgot that I couldn't hear them if I wasn't looking at them, but trust me, that is one thing I would never forget. "With you or me?"

"If you want it you can have it," Needles said when I looked at him again.

"What?" We were still working on lip reading.

If you want the appointment it's yours. Doesn't matter to me, he signed and shrugged again. I just nodded then headed back to the smaller rooms we used for tattooing. Needles had a great set up here. Each of the artists had their own space that was sectioned off into rooms with no doors, and for the most part all the artists stayed out of each other's space.

I was hanging out in my studio when a ball of paper flew into my line of vision. I wasn't sure how long I had been sitting there drawing but the sudden appearance of flying paper surprised me. I looked up and found Ashlyn standing in the doorway.

"Sorry," she said with a little wave. "I've been waiting for a while."

"Where's Needles?" I asked, mostly catching what she said.

"I don't know," She said shrugging.

"He probably went to the back and forgot to turn on the flashers." I said, shrugging as I stood and walked towards her.

"Flashers?" She frowned slightly and it was damn cute.

"Lights that flash when someone comes in the front door," I said, directing her to the front desk where my sketch book was. "I don't have to hear them."

"Oh," she replied

"Are you here alone?"

"No," she said shaking her head and motioning to the back, "Pixie went to find Needles."

"Pixie went to find Needles?" I asked and she nodded. "Ok, my lip reading isn't so great yet so I might repeat what you've said, sorry."

"It's ok," she said, shrugging again. "Is there something I can do to make it easier?"

"Easier?" I asked and she nodded again. "Write?"

"Sure," she replied smiling. She pulled my sketch pad to her and started writing then passed me the book as she pulled out a drawing.

I want a tattoo that symbolizes my sister and finding her after seventeen years, this is what I was thinking.

I took the drawing from her and was blown away by the amount of detail and creativity. It was a small stylized pixie reaching for the stars. Usually anything drawn stylized is black and white, but this pixie was drawn in rainbow colours.

"Did you draw this?" I asked, she nodded shyly, "It's amazing, you're super talented. Where did you want to put it?" She smiled at the compliment and pointed to the back of her shoulder. "It'll look awesome there, is there anything else you were thinking of?"

Ashlyn giggled and I figured I was talking too loud again, but I couldn't help it. She shook her head no and started writing again.

I noticed in your sketchbook that you are also very talented, what would you add?

"I don't know, but you want this pixie to look like your sister right?" She nodded and shrugged, "I could make your pixie look more like your sister if you want."

She nodded again and started writing once again.

You kept my notes from the other day, why?

"I could say it was because it had your name and number on it for

Needles, but really it was because I like your writing. It's very pretty." Ashlyn blushed again and ducked her head just as Pixie joined us again.

They talked a few minutes more and Pixie signed instead of wrote which was better since I didn't want her to see her sister's notes and then they left after making an appointment for the weekend for Ashlyn to get her pixie done.

"Did you know Ashlyn's an artist?" I called to Needles; he shook his head no so I kept talking about Ashlyn. "She designed her tat, it's really well done. If you're still looking for women to work here you should tap her. She'd probably be really good."

He tapped me on the shoulder to get my attention then signed, *what's your interest in this girl? You know she's not legal yet right?*

"Yeah I know, she's hot but I'm not stupid. I can wait a year or so." I replied, shaking my head. "I'm only twenty, not like there's a huge age difference, but yeah, I'll wait."

"Good," he said and nodded.

Ashlyn

"Holy sis, what is going on with you and Lix?" Pixie asked when we were back in my car. She had her driver's license but not a vehicle and she didn't want to drive Seether's giant truck. She said riding in it was one thing, driving it was something totally different.

"I don't know," I said, shrugging, trying not to make too big a deal about it. "He's a nice guy, he's going to do my tattoo."

"He's super freaking hot!" she exclaimed, turning in her seat to face me.

"Yeah, he's good looking."

"Oh please, he's super freaking hot, admit it."

"Ok, I admit it," I said as I turned on the main road to her house. "He's super freaking hot. But that doesn't mean anything."

"Sure it does, besides he was just as into you."

"Really?" I asked, totally interested now.

"Oh yeah, even Needles noticed it." Pixie nodded smiling wickedly at me.

"You're not just saying that are you?"

"Are you kidding? I just found you again; do you really think I would do something like that?"

"No, you're right, I'm sorry. I'm just not very good at these things. Dad kept me pretty sheltered and I've only ever been on one date and that did not go very well."

"What happened?"

"I was so nervous I didn't say a word and then when he dropped me off he actually shook my hand and then the next day at school told all his friends that I was boring." I said sullenly.

That really had been a horrible couple of weeks before another scandal rocked the school in typical teenage fashion and I was off the hook.

"Oh sweetie, I'm sorry." Pixie said touching my arm. "Are you nervous around Lix?"

"Huh," I muttered as I thought about it. "Yes but no, like I'm not so nervous that I can't think of anything to say, but nervous that I hope he likes me too sort of thing."

"Makes sense," Pixie nodded. I loved my sister; she was always supportive and wonderful. "You should call him."

"What!" I demanded as I pulled into the driveway of the house she shared with Seether, almost running over her garbage can. "I can't call him!"

"Why not, what would it hurt?" she asked innocently, then smiled, "Just think about it." She gave me a hug and slid out of the car, running inside, waving as she went.

I backed out of the driveway and drove home. My step mom was home but she was somewhere in the back of the house and didn't hear me come in. I loved Leticia like the flighty step mother she was.

She was so pure and simple and always made everything seem so easy. She never over thought things and her whole world seemed to be sunshine and roses.

I rushed up to my room and sat on the edge of my bed just as my phone chimed with a text message. Probably Pixie I thought. I took my phone out of my purse and opened it up. There was a strange number with a message underneath.

**Hey, it's Lix, just wanted to say hi, hope it's
ok that I copied your number from
the note you left Needles.**

Oh holy shit!! What the hell did I say? Lix was texting me? He just wanted to say hi? Is that code for something?

**Honestly if this isn't ok just say so and
I will leave you alone.**

That was the next message. Oh shit! I had taken too long to answer! Crap! What did I say?

No, it's fine, great. Hi

Shit I was an idiot.

Lol, hi. I really do like your drawing for your tattoo

**Um, thanks, I've always wanted a tattoo but
Of course I only turn 18 in August and never knew**

Where to go to get one

Makes sense, so you turn 18 next month?

Uh, yeah on the 26th.

Cool, I guess I can wait that long.

Wait that long for what?

Lol, you

Now I was really confused. Why would he have to wait for me?

I don't get it....

Have coffee with me tomorrow and I'll explain

Oh shit! Now what?

Ok, when and where?

The Esquires on the highway? 11?

Sure, sounds good, meet you there?

Yup, see you there, can't wait ;)

A wink emoji? What the hell did that mean? Shit I was in trouble. I immediately called my sister.

CHAPTER 3

Lix

So, I asked her out. Why not right? She was hot, she was cute, I really liked what I knew about her. I really hoped the feeling was mutual. I guess we would see soon right? I was sitting outside the Esquires waiting.

I was about half an hour early but I didn't care, I wanted to get there first. That only made me nervous though, waiting, thinking she was late then checking my phone for a brush off text only to see that I had to wait another fifteen minutes. Shit.

At five minutes to eleven a silver Honda Civic sedan pulled into the spot beside my old truck. Yes I was in an MC but I didn't ride a bike. I had worked too hard as a kid to save up for that truck and I wasn't ready to give it up yet.

Ashlyn stepped out of the car with her purse then closed the door and skipped up to the sidewalk where I was standing waiting. She smiled hugely at me and I think she said hi.

"How are you?" I asked stupidly.

Good, she signed.

"You're learning sign language?" I asked happily. She nodded and shrugged then signed *easier* and mimicked writing. "Got it," I nodded then motioned for her to precede me into the coffee shop then motioned for her to order before me and pulled out my wallet.

I haven't got a clue what she ordered and I was too busy staring at her to notice. I ordered a large black coffee and we moved to the pickup spot.

We stood for a few minutes then she got excited and started digging in her purse. She smiled again as she pulled out a notebook and a cutesy pen. She made a big show and flourish of opening the book and clicking the pen before she started writing then handed the book to me.

Until I know more sign language, I thought having a notebook would help.

"I like it." I said nodding and smiling at her like an idiot. I was about to say something else when she motioned at two cups that had appeared on the counter beside me. We took our drinks and walked outside to sit on the sidewalk.

So, what did you mean yesterday about waiting for me?

"Ah, well," I said and ducked my head. "You're not legal yet, and I'm past legal and I would really like to date you but I would rather neither of us get in trouble."

"Oh," she said blushing then pulling her notebook closer to herself.

I've never dated anyone before. Are you sure you want to date me?

"Fuck yes I'm sure!" I barked a laugh. "You're smart, funny and beautiful, why wouldn't I want to date you?" She made a motion to shush me and I figured I was probably yelling again. "Sorry, can't hear myself."

She nodded smiling then started writing.

Ok, I'm going to be completely honest, I have absolutely no experience; I don't know what I'm doing?

I looked at that last note for a few minutes before I looked up into her pretty gray eyes. She was obviously so nervous and worried I hated she felt that way.

"I am not going to ask you to do anything you're not comfortable with." I said reaching out and taking her hand. "I want to date you, get to know you, talk to you. If that leads to more than great, if it doesn't that's fine, I can live with just being your friend. I want more, but I'm not going to push you into anything you're not ready for."

She frowned at me for a few seconds before writing again.

It might take me a long time, but I want to get to know you, too and I think I would like more than friendship, but let's start with that first?

"Sounds good sweetheart," I said smiling at her as she bit her bottom lip. "I'm good with that," but I reached out and pulled her lip from between her teeth with my thumb.

She smiled and blushed, ducking her head as I pulled my hand back. We talked for a few hours more and I thought we would fill that notebook with her notes. I taught her some sign language and we laughed when she messed it up.

I looked quickly at my phone and swore.

"Shit, I gotta go to work," I said shaking my head. "I'm sorry I lost track of time."

"It's ok," she said smiling and gathering up her things. I stood beside the table and grabbed our two cups, long since empty and tossed them in the garbage. She stood looking up at me for a second before we both started to talk at once.

"Sorry," I said ducking my head, "You first."

She smiled and signed *good* and *time.* I smiled down at her.

"You had a good time?" She nodded gazing up at me, no artifice in her face. "Me too."

"What were you going to say?" She asked tipping her head to the side.

"I was going to ask you if I could kiss you." I said matter of fact. Her eyes widened and she blushed but smiled then nodded slightly. I smiled hugely and stepped closer to her, skimming my hand under her hair and tipping her chin up with my thumb. She was pretty tall, only a few inches shorter than me and she was a perfect height for me to just dip my head and touch my lips to hers.

I closed my eyes and savoured the feel of her against me as the hand I had placed at her waist pulled her closer to me as I deepened the kiss just slightly. I didn't want to scare her but I had to taste her.

I opened my mouth slightly over hers and touched her lips with my tongue, making her gasp. I opened my eyes to see her expression but her eyes were closed as her mouth dropped open just slightly so I licked inside just a little, just a taste. The sweet sound she made was enough to make me just a little hard but I had to pull back before I frightened her.

I rested my forehead against hers then kissed her lightly again on the lips. Her hands were gripping my biceps and I could feel her breath tickling my chin as she nibbled that lip again. I smoothed over the little teeth marks with my thumb and kissed them then pulled back, taking her hand in mine and staring down into her eyes.

"Wow."

Ashlyn

Wow is right! I mean, as far as first kisses go, not that I'm an expert or anything, having only been kissed once, that was pretty amazing! Holy shit! Ok, I've got to calm down or I'm going to get into an accident. I pushed a button on my steering wheel and told Siri to call Pixie.

"Hey sista! How was coffee?" Pixie answered.

"He kissed me!" I squealed as I stopped at a red light. I looked in my rear view mirror as his truck roared away in the opposite direction.

"Really? Was it amazing?" Pixie asked, sounding just as excited as I was.

"Oh yeah, it was amazing!"

"I've been talking to Aiden about Lix; he says Lix is a really great guy." Pixie said getting a bit serious now. "Do you know how he lost his hearing?"

"An IED that caused a brain injury," I replied nodding and biting my lip even though she couldn't see me. "He said he's got a lot of ringing in his ears."

"Yeah, that's got to drive a guy nuts!" Pixie exclaimed, then quieter, "Baby wait, I'm talking to Ash."

"It's ok Pix; go be with Aiden, I'll talk to you later." I said chuckling.

"Are you sure? Aiden can wait. Stop it, yes you can."

"No he can't, you're trying to get pregnant, go be with your fiancé." I laughed again and shook my head and said goodbye and hung up. I really wished I had lots of girlfriends that I could call but my shyness didn't just extend to guys, I was shy around everyone.

I rushed home and was happy to see that my dad's car was in the driveway. I parked my own car and ran inside, finding him in his study.

"Daddy, I have to talk to you." I said plopping myself on the leather couch in his office and turning to put my feet on the couch.

"Mmhmm," He murmured.

"No Daddy, really I have to talk to you right now." I said turning to lean up on my elbow and look at him over the arm of the couch.

"What is it sweetheart?"

"You have to put down the pen, Daddy."

"What? Oh, sure." My dad was pretty awesome. Sometimes it took him a few minutes to let go of the dentistry magazines but when he did he was attentive and kind. Now he stood from behind his desk and walked over to sit on one of the arm chairs opposite the couch. "What did you want to talk about?"

"I met someone." I said smiling, waiting for his reaction. It took him a second to react then he nodded and pursed his lips. "He's a bit older."

"How much older is a bit?"

"He's twenty."

"Where did you meet him?"

"Um, he works at the tattoo parlor that the War Angel's own." I said nervously. This was the part that might just set my dad off.

"Is he part of the club?"

"Yeah, he said today he was the first vet to go through their new program." I said, trying to remember every word he said today. "He doesn't consider himself a vet though because he only did one tour and came back pretty quickly injured."

"How was he injured?"

"Um, and IED I'm pretty sure he said. He said he hit his head when the truck rolled and he got a brain injury that causes ringing in his ears." I said feeling a little more confident that dad was going to be open minded.

"You haven't told me this boy's name yet."

"Oh, it's Felix but he goes by Lix."

"Does he have any family?" Dad was sitting back in the chair now, completely relaxed.

"Yup, he has three older sisters and a bunch of nieces and nephews. He said they all live down in Kelowna."

"I have to tell you Ashlyn, I never planned on being a dad when my sister died. When I got the call that her kids needed someone to adopt them I jumped to go and get you. And then when Sylvia said she would only take you I was heartbroken. I think though that over the years you have grown into an amazing young woman. I believe that you are smart and you have a good head on your shoulders.

"I know you're not going to rush into anything but I also know you don't have a lot of experience. A guy, even a twenty year old one usually has a whole lot more experience than girls the same age. Just be careful, and make sure you bring him over to meet us very soon."

I couldn't help it; I smiled so big I felt like my cheeks were going to crack. I jumped up from the couch and kissed my dad on the cheek then ran up to my room. I was just plugging my phone into the charger when a message came through

I had a good time today, can we do it again soon?

Hell yes we could do it again soon!!!

**Sure, it's Thursday and I'm going to be in
The shop on Saturday, do you want to wait**

Until then?

Not if I don't have to.

Oh, ok. What did you have in mind?

I have to work most of the day tomorrow
How about a movie?

Sure, I like most anything, you pick.

What if I picked a horror movie?

**Um, ok but you'll have to protect me from
The scary parts.**

Why else would I pick a horror movie?

You're bad.

Lol, yup.
Customer just walked in, gotta go ttys

Ttys

Oh my God! I needed girlfriends! How did people do this without totally losing their minds? This was too exciting and the only person I could really talk to was having sex with her fiancé. Shit!

Lix was going to want that eventually. I know he said he would push me into anything but still. Did I want that?

Hell yeah, I think I definitely did want that. Not tomorrow, but soon. It was the middle of July; I would like that by my birthday I think.

Lix texted later that evening with the name and time of a movie, thank God it wasn't a horror, I don't think I could handle that, even if he was there to protect me. I had to look the movie up, Atomic Blonde, ok I could watch that, or cuddle up with a hot guy in a theater while it was on the screen, whatever.

I did tell him that he had to pick me up and meet my dad. Lix said that wasn't a problem and he would be happy to meet my dad as long as my dad knew Lix couldn't hear him.

I said not to worry about it then thought again about where we were going tomorrow night. Why was Lix taking me to the movies if he couldn't hear it?

CHAPTER 4

Lix

I was early again. The movie started at 7:30 and I told Ashlyn I would pick her up at 6:30 so we'd have time to get from her dad's place to the theater on the other side of town and I could chat with her dad for a few minutes and we wouldn't be worried about missing the movie. I looked at the clock on the dash of my truck, 6:00, I was way early.

I almost jumped out of my skin when there was a knock on the driver's side window of the truck. I looked out the window to find Ashlyn standing there smiling so I rolled the window down.

"What are you doing?" She asked, smiling sweetly.

"Don't know, nervous I guess." I said shrugging and smiling back at her. "How did you know I was here?"

"Your music is really loud." She pointed to the stereo of the truck and I realized it was turned up almost as loud as it would go.

"Oh!" I reached over and turned it off then sat looking at her.

"Are you going to come in?"

"Ah sure," I said and reached for the door handle but she stopped me.

"You might want to turn the truck off." I didn't catch everything she said but she pointed at my keys and I realized my mistake.

"Shit." I cursed under my breath. I turned off the truck, took a few deep breaths then got out of the truck. I stood in front of her and smiled knowing what a complete idiot I was. I did the only thing I could think of that would make me feel better.

I leaned forward and captured her lips with mine and kissed her. I hadn't planned it to be more than a sweet peck but she opened her mouth and licked my lips and I couldn't help myself.

I reached up and cupped her jaw with both of my hands and held her close as I plundered her mouth. I groaned and pulled back breathing hard. She tapped my shoulder and I felt a giggle in her throat. Ashlyn pointed over my shoulder and I turned to see her dad standing in the front doorway of the house.

"Shit," I said again then took her hand and walked up the walk to the front door. "Mr. Cameron." I said, extending my hand to shake his.

"Felix," Ashlyn's dad said, shaking my hand with a firm grip. "Please come inside."

I followed Mr. Cameron into the house and Ashlyn walked beside me. I saw her lips moving like she was talking to her dad but I didn't catch what she said. I frowned and looked from her to his back as he walked away from me. I tugged on her hand to get her attention and when she looked up at me I asked her "what's up?"

"Dad's being rude." She replied, rolling her eyes. Then she turned sharply and said something to her dad but again I missed it. From the look on her face I'd say her voice was raised now and she was angry as she spoke to her dad. She seemed to listen for a minute then shook her head and I read "We're leaving," on her lips.

I turned with Ashlyn ready to walk out the front door and find out what was going on but she stopped abruptly and waited facing forward and not moving. Finally after what seemed like forever she turned to me and smiled slightly her cheeks read.

"Dad says he's sorry he was rude." She said but I shook my head because I still only got dad and rude. She put her pointer finger up and rushed away then came back with a pad of paper and a pen.

Dad says he's sorry he was rude.

I frowned at her and lifted my eyebrows in question because I still didn't know what was going on.

He was purposely facing away from you and talking to you at the same time, knowing you couldn't hear him.

I smirked at his little joke and turned to him but still spoke to Ashlyn, "As long as he doesn't mind me purposefully ignoring him by accident sometimes."

Mr. Cameron threw his head back and seemed to be laughing. I could just imagine the deep sound of his laugh reverberating through the house.

Ashlyn

I couldn't believe my dad was being so rude, but I suppose it was a test of sorts. I think Lix passed with flying colours, not taking offense and making a joke out of it. We talked for a few more minutes with my dad then I looked pointedly at my watch.

"Well, I guess we should be going." I smiled up at Lix and he just smiled back, knowing exactly what I was doing. Slowly he turned to my dad and held his hand out again.

"It was a pleasure meeting you, sir," he said waiting for my dad to take his hand.

"You as well son, take care of my girl." Dad said, shaking Lix's hand firmly.

"Absolutely sir," Lix said then led me out of the house. At the truck he held the door for me then ran around to the other side and climbed in. Once he started the truck he reached for the radio but I stopped his hand and he gave me a strange look.

"Can you hear the radio?" I asked him, pointing first at the radio then my ear.

"No," He said, shaking his head then chuckled and shrugged, "Habit I guess. Do you want the radio on?"

"No," I said shaking my head and smiling then took a deep breath. "Why are we going to a movie if you can't hear it?"

He shrugged, "I can still watch it, if I like what I see then I can buy it and watch it with subtitles." He said finally smiling, "Besides, I get to sit in a dark theater with a pretty girl beside me, I might not watch the movie at all." I blushed at that and rolled my eyes but was actually quite pleased.

When we got to the theater Lix paid for our tickets and we decided to get something to eat after the movie so we just got drinks. I don't know if Lix watched much of the movie but he either held my hand or had his arm around my shoulder the whole time.

I think the movie was pretty good but I was distracted by the little circles Lix was drawing either on my hand or the back of my neck. At one point I shivered from the combination of Lix's fingers and the air conditioning and he rubbed his thumb across my neck a little harder, leaving what felt like a trail of fire.

The movie ended and we sat through the credits as everyone else was up and leaving as quickly as they could. Lix turned in his seat and watched my face.

"Am I yelling?" He asked, he actually wasn't but the question struck me as funny so I giggled as I shook my head no. "Good, I'd hate for the entire theater to know how much I like holding you."

I blushed again and giggled then pointed to myself and held up two fingers. He smiled then looked around the theater. It was finally empty so he took my hand and led me out and to his truck. When we got to it he turned me to lean back against it and leaned into me, kissing me gently.

"Are you hungry?" he asked, rubbing his thumbs up and down my sides. I shrugged because I wasn't hungry for an actual meal but wouldn't mind something sweet. "Is this twenty questions?" Lix laughed.

"I could go for dessert." I said smiling up at him and running my hands up his biceps to his shoulders. He smiled wickedly and lowered his head to mine, kissing me long and deep, his tongue twisting with mine.

"You are dessert." He said quietly as he pulled away then kissed me quick, "Come on, we'll get ice cream at Dairy Queen, sound good?"

I nodded and smiled then climbed into the truck. Lix turned on the truck and reached for the radio again then stopped chuckling to himself. We got to the Dairy Queen and ordered our ice cream then sat by the window, enjoying the cold treat and cool air conditioning.

"Did you add anything to my tattoo?" I asked him then put some ice cream in my mouth. He was already watching my mouth to read my lips but he seemed to get distracted by me licking the spoon clean.

"Uh, your tattoo?" He asked, shaking his head a bit as if to clear it. "Yeah, I asked Pixie when you guys met each other again and added that date as well and both your birthdays in the wings and had to adjust the wings just a bit to accommodate the dates. I added a butterfly and a bower of daffodils because both mean new beginnings, like your relationship is starting new."

"That sounds amazing," I said but Lix wasn't looking at me. I dug in my purse for a pen and grabbed a napkin and wrote him a note.

I can't talk to you if you don't look at me. I wrote and slipped the napkin under his gaze. He read it and chuckled then looked up at me sheepishly.

"Sorry," he said shrugging, "I guess talking about my art is still kind of . . . strange. No one ever wanted to talk about it before."

I held up a finger and rushed to the front of the restaurant where the napkin bar was. I grabbed a handful and rushed back then started writing again.

This is easier than trying to guess what I'm saying, I wrote and smiled. We filled the notebook so I have to go buy another one, at least until I learn more sign language.

"Haha, that's true," Lix said smiling, "Besides, I like your writing, it's as pretty as you are."

We sat like that for hours again, me writing on napkins and both of us laughing. A few times he got too loud and I had to shush him and he just laughed harder. I swear we went through a whole industrial sized package of napkins that night.

Eventually we realized the restaurant was empty and the staff were mopping the floor and stocking empty containers, guess it was time for us to go.

It was still warm out, even though it was well after midnight. Again Lix pushed me up against the passenger door of his truck and kissed me like he might die without me.

I pushed my hands into his hair and he very properly kept his hands high on my back. When he couldn't help but stop to take a breath he pulled back just enough that our lips parted.

"I hope I'm whispering right now 'cause if I'm yelling that would totally kill the mood." He panted slightly, I smiled and nodded because it was close enough to a whisper. "I know it hasn't been very long, like not even a week that we've known each other but

I knew the second I saw you that you were special, that I had to have you."

Before I could say anything he was kissing me again, molding me to him as he tasted and teased. Damn, I was really falling for Lix, even before he said that. Now I was going to fall hard and fast for him and I sure hoped he didn't hurt me.

CHAPTER 5

Lix

I was sitting in my chair working on Ashlyn's tattoo the next day. When I showed her what I had added to it she had almost started to cry. I'm pretty sure they were happy tears but had to guess by her smile. She nodded and turned her back, pulling her shirt off then pulled the strap of her bra down her arm.

"Whoa, stop," I chuckled, "I have something for you to wear."

"This was as far as I was going," I think she said as she laughed. When she laughed it was harder to read her lips.

"Here," I handed her a big button up shirt with short sleeves, "put this on backwards in the bathroom. I need you to take your bra off too, sorry."

"That's ok," She chuckled again, taking the shirt and walking into the bathroom. When she came out I had all my things set up and a chair turned for her to sit on so her shoulder would be at the perfect height and position. I had been working for quite some time when Needles came in.

He sat and chatted with Ash but I didn't pay any attention to their conversation. I was far too preoccupied with the tattoo, at one point I lifted the tattoo gun to wipe Ashlyn's shoulder clean and she shrugged at something they were talking about. Shortly after that Needles got up and walked out of the room and to the main part of the store.

It didn't take me much time after that to finish Ash's ink, maybe twenty minutes. I wiped it clean, put cream on it and covered it then kissed the spot, telling her she could get dressed but be careful with her bra rubbing.

She smiled over her shoulder then walked into the bathroom. When she came back I must have been in the back cleaning my stuff up because when I got back the bathroom was empty and she wasn't in my room.

I figured Ashlyn was in the front talking to Needles so I didn't worry about it much. It wasn't until he came back looking like he was about to fall over that I started to worry.

I've got a migraine coming on, he signed looking weary. *Ashlyn said she'd stay and help with the front, call in another guy if you need to. Siobhan is taking me home.*

Then he turned and was gone. I watched him frowning as Ash came back into the room. I had only ever seen Needles have a migraine once before. He said they were a result of his past heroin use and he just had to suffer through them since he couldn't take anything for the pain. I shook my head wishing I could do more to help.

Ashlyn

"Ash, Lix here said you might want to become an artist?" Needles said, suddenly watching me. Lix wasn't paying any attention to us but I was pretty sure he was just about finished my tattoo. He had been at it for quite a while.

"Um, I've been thinking about it," I said, shrugging slightly as Lix took the needle away from my shoulder to wipe the area clean. "I love to draw; I just don't know how good I'd be at the tattooing part."

"It definitely takes practice." Needles said thoughtfully as the chime above the door went off. "Think about it, I'd like to see some of your art, maybe you can start off just designing and working the front. But you're under eighteen so I need to know that your dad is ok with you working here."

"All done," Lix said a few minutes after Needles left. He had put cream or something on the area and covered it with plastic then kissed my shoulder. I smiled at him happily. "You can go back into the bathroom and change, just be careful of your bra strap rubbing the tat. Leave that strap off if you can."

I did what Lix said and when I came out he was gone and I heard angry voices coming from the front of the store. Then the bells above the door jangled again and it was quiet.

"Come on, I'll take you home so you can get some sleep." I heard a woman say as I stepped into the main area of the shop.

"I can't leave; Lix has got a full schedule." Needles said, shaking his head.

I cleared my throat and both Needles and a very pretty, short blonde turned to look at me.

"I can stay and help Lix," I said smiling shyly. "Um, maybe a sort of trial run to see if I want to work here? Or to see if I can do it and you really want me to work here?"

Needles nodded and started towards the back room. "I'll just tell Lix the plan then and call in another guy to help out."

"I'm Siobhan," the blonde said smiling slightly. She said her name like Sha-vaughn and held out her hand.

"I'm Ashlyn, I'm Pixie's sister." I said, shaking Siobhan's hand. "It's nice to meet you."

"Did you just get a tattoo done?"

"Uh, yeah, Lix just put a pixie on my shoulder." I nodded and moved the edge of my shirt to show her.

"Oh so cool! He did a really good job! Did Lix draw it, too?"

"Uh, parts of it, the daffodil and the butterfly and he put the dates in the wings but the rest I did." I replied shrugging.

"Wow, you are really talented. I would love for you to design something for me someday."

"Oh, I'd love to! You should talk to Alana over at the MC, too." I said smiling and getting excited, "She sometimes designs for Needles."

"Oh, I'll do that! I'm sure she'll be over there tonight and if I'm there with Jaxon tonight I'll probably run into her. I've been looking forward to meeting her."

"Oh she's great," I said, waving a bit just as Needles came back into the front space.

"See ya, Ash," he said and Siobhan waved.

"So, you're working with me, hey?" I turned to see Lix in the doorway, leaning against the jamb with his arms folded over his chest and his ankles crossed.

"I guess I am," I said happily and smiled. "I just met Siobhan, she's nice."

"Siobhan, she's nice, hey?" Lix asked, smiling and walking towards me. I giggled knowing he probably didn't catch everything I said. When he was standing right in front of me he leaned over and trapped me against the counter. "I guess I should show you how to use the cash register hey?"

"You can, but I have a better idea," I said and reached up on my toes, fitting my lips to his. He quickly took over and licked my lips, pushing his tongue into my mouth and dueling with my tongue.

We stayed like that, tasting and sipping at each other until the bells over the door rang and I pulled away and turned within the cage of Lix's arms. I smiled at the person who came through the door as Lix dropped his head to my shoulder, breathing heavy.

CHAPTER 6

Ashlyn

Over the last month Lix and I had spent every chance together that we could. I had started working at WAMC Tat's and loved it. Needles was really good about giving Lix and me most of our days off together so we really did see each other every day and then we texted pretty much all night.

I had gotten much better with my sign language and Lix and I rarely used a notebook anymore but I kind of missed it so I still wrote him notes once in a while.

Tomorrow was my birthday, I was finally eighteen. I had never really cared about age much before, but since Lix and I started seeing each other and getting to know each other I was really chomping at the bit.

Lix was good on his promise and never pressured me for anything and even though we kissed and the petting got pretty heavy he never went farther than I was comfortable with. I was actually ready to go farther much sooner than my birthday but I knew he wasn't comfortable with me being underage so I had to content myself to wait, but only until tomorrow.

My birthday this year fell on a Saturday and I had the day off. I was spending it with my quite pregnant sister. Pixie had found out a few weeks ago that she was finally expecting and that she was already three months along.

She was barely showing but she was loving everything about it. She said she couldn't feel the baby yet but everything else was so glorious. She didn't have morning sickness and she hoped that meant good things. I didn't know anything about babies or being pregnant so I was going to take her word for it.

Now we were lying on matching massage tables as a couple of women rubbed all the stiff and sore muscles out of our bodies. Pixie was almost asleep; she was so relaxed; I had to laugh at her.

"Is Lix taking you out tonight?" she asked suddenly, barely moving her lips to speak.

"Yeah, but I don't know what he has planned." I replied smiling. "He just said to come here and relax and beautify."

"He's such an awesome guy," Pixie said with a moan as her masseuse worked on a particularly tough spot. "You should definitely keep him around."

"Oh I plan on it." I said, and then all conversation stopped as we enjoyed our pampering. After the massages we had mani/pedi's and got our hair done. It was a perfect day and a perfect way to spend time with my sister.

I had told Lix to pick me up at Pixie and Seether's house instead of driving all the way up to my dad's house. He thought that was a pretty good idea since then he could hang out with Seether for a few minutes while he waited for me.

I found him sitting in the living room with Seether with the TV on but they didn't seem to be watching it, instead they were signing, or rather Seether was signing and Lix was talking, loudly. Seether didn't care; he was probably used to it by now.

When I stepped into the living room Seether stopped signing mid-sentence and just stared. It took Lix a minute but he finally realized that Seether had stopped for a reason and looked in the direction Seether was looking.

Lix's gaze settled on me and he stood slowly from his chair then let his eyes roam from my head to my toes and back again. Finally his eyes met mine and he took a sharp breath through his teeth.

"Wow," he exhaled and stepped towards me. "You look amazing." I smiled up at him and lifted my hands to sign.

Thank you, you look pretty good yourself. And he did, he was wearing new dark jeans and a black button down dress shirt. It looked like he had even polished his boots. I had dressed up for him, too.

After our day at the spa, Pixie and I had gone shopping. I had found a cute but sexy little black dress that was light and summery and paired it with black flip flops that were a little bit fancy. Of course it wasn't the dress that I was excited about, it was the fancy underwear I had on underneath.

"You ready," Lix asked, taking my hand in his. I nodded and he leaned down and kissed me gently. "Bye guys."

"What's the plan?" I asked, tugging on his hand to get his attention.

"Dinner, then dancing." He replied smiling.

"Dancing?"

"You'll see." And I did. Dinner was wonderful, Lix took me to a semi-fancy restaurant that served amazing food and was close to the river. When we finished eating it was just starting to get dark but it was still nice enough out that we decided to walk along the river and watch the gulls play in the water.

Is this the dancing part? I asked pointing at the birds swooping and diving.

"No," He chuckled, shaking his head. "Come on, I'll show you." Lix dragged me back to his truck and drove us out to an empty field on the way to the War Angels clubhouse. We got out and he leaned back in to turn on the radio then took me in his arms and swayed from side to side. "I'm not much of a dancer."

"You're perfect," I said staring up into his eyes. I lifted up on my toes and kissed him softly then rested my head under his chin on his chest. We swayed with the breeze for a long time, totally not in time to the music but it didn't matter, I was with Lix and he was holding me in his arms and that's all that mattered.

Finally I couldn't wait any longer; I looked up at him and cupped his cheek, making him tilt his head until he was looking down at me.

"Take me home." I said as clearly as I could so he could read my lips.

"You want to go home?"

I shook my head and took a step back, freeing my hands. *Take me to your home; I want you to be my birthday gift tonight.*

Lix

"Are you saying what I think you're saying?" I asked her, going completely still. I was hoping I was right and she was telling me she was ready to be completely mine but I wasn't going to rush her. She nodded yes and reached up and kissed me again. "Are you sure? You don't have to, we don't have to, I didn't expect that."

I want to, please Lix we've waited long enough. She was starting to look worried, like I would say no, but there was no way in hell I was going to say no to her.

"Ok, let's go then but it hardly seems fair that it's your birthday and I get to unwrap the most precious gift." I said nodding.

I helped her into the truck then ran around to the other side and got in. My truck was older and had a bench seat so I grabbed her and pulled her over to sit next to me. I put the truck in gear and peeled out of the field as fast as I could.

When we got to the clubhouse there were a few trucks and bikes in the parking lot so I pulled around the back and used my key to let us in the hallway instead of going through the main room.

I didn't want Ashlyn embarrassed and I really wanted her all to myself. If we had gone through the main room someone would have seen her and insisted she hang out for her birthday.

Holding her hand I pulled her behind me to my room and unlocked my door then closed it behind us and locked it again. I stood staring at her, leaning against the door, waiting for her to give me some sign as to what she wanted or needed.

She turned to me and smiled, holding out her hand. We had been in my room before just talking or fooling around but now it seemed strange. I wondered how we had so much self-control.

I took her hand and pulled her to me gently, skimming my hands up her bare arms and cupping her shoulders, then took the straps of her dress and pulled them down her arms letting them trap her arms at her elbows.

The top of the dress still covered her breasts but just barely and I could just see the lace edge of her bra. I leaned forward and kissed her lips, coaxing her tongue out to play.

Ashlyn pulled her arms out of the straps of her dress and wrapped them around my neck, tugging the hair at my nape. I put my hands on the flesh of her waist that had been bared when she'd pulled her arms out and pushed them up to play with the clasp of her bra.

"Wait," she said pulling away, "I want to show you something." She stepped back and pushed her dress off her hips and down her legs. She stood in front of me wearing nothing but her underwear and I almost swallowed my tongue. She looked spectacular, her bra black lace that pushed her beautiful breast up high and her panties a matching lace thong.

"I was right," I said, not able to drag my gaze from her, "I do get to open the best present."

You have too many clothes on, she signed smiling slyly.

I quickly whipped my shirt over my head and dropped it on the floor then toed my boots off. Ashlyn's hands quickly reached up and molded around the muscles in my chest then she dragged her nails down my abs and buried her fingers in the waistband of my jeans.

I held her wrists and kissed her again, walking her back to the bed. When the backs of her knees hit the mattress she sat down but kept her hands wrapped in my waistband.

I undid the button and zipper of my jeans and pushed them off my hips and down my legs, leaving my underwear on but pulling off my socks. I leaned over her, urging her to move farther up the bed.

When her head touched the pillow I laid over her, my hip cocked and my knee pushing her leg up and rubbing against her center. With one hand on her stomach I leaned over and kissed her throat and chest, sucking her sweet skin. Her hands weren't still, but coasted over my back and down my arms.

I reached around her and undid the clasp of her bra, pulling it down her arms and tossing it on the floor then cupped one of her breasts and brought the nipple to my mouth, pushing it with my tongue to the roof of my mouth and sucking hard. Ashlyn arched off the bed and dug her nails into my bicep. I kissed down her torso, swirling my tongue around her belly button then went lower and kissed her mound through her panties.

I looked up at her as I teased the edges of her panties with a finger, sliding it just under to gently rub the lips of her pussy. Her panties were already wet and I could smell her arousal.

I wished I could hear the sounds she was making but I would have to be satisfied with feeling her, tasting her, smelling her. I pulled the thong off of her and tossed it after her bra then buried my face in her pussy and moaned.

Ashlyn tried to close her legs but I wouldn't let her and pushed her thighs wider with my shoulders. She might have whimpered and I looked up at her to make sure she was ok and she stared at me, apprehension in her eyes.

"Please can I?" I asked, rubbing my thumb over the silky skin of her inner thigh. She nodded slowly and bit her bottom lip. "You'll like it, I promise." Ashlyn nodded again, more sure this time.

I flattened my tongue over her, licking her from her opening to her clit and swirling my tongue around her sensitive nub.

She arched again as I sucked her clit into my mouth then gently pushed a finger inside her. She was so damn tight I didn't know how I was going to fit my cock into her.

I rubbed her inner walls, stretching her then inserting another finger with the first and spread them wide. I kept sucking and pumping my fingers as I felt her muscles contract around my fingers and her thighs started to quiver.

"Let go baby, let me have it." I licked her again and she came hard around my fingers and writhed under my tongue.

Finally when she started to relax a little I sat up and pushed my boxers off then reached over and pulled a condom from my night stand.

As I ripped the foil packet with my teeth I rubbed her clit with the thumb of my other hand, not wanting her to lose that loose relaxed feeling.

I fit the condom over my aching cock and positioned the head at her opening then looked her in the eyes.

"Are you ready?" I asked, rubbing her nose with mine.

Ashlyn nodded and smiled slightly. I kissed her hard, mimicking with my tongue what I was going to do with my cock then drove into her, not stopping until I was fully seated. When I was as far as I could go I stopped and pulled my mouth from hers, leaving a trail of kisses over her face.

"Are you ok?"

Ashlyn nodded slightly, then shook her head no as a tear escaped her closed eyes. Shit, I hurt her, I knew it would hurt the first time but I had hoped I had prepared her enough for my invasion.

CHAPTER 7

Ashlyn

Damn that hurt. Lix had been so good, preparing me, stretching me. I knew that was what he was doing, I thought I was ready for his intrusion but I was wrong. I wanted to be strong, I didn't want him to see my cry, but I couldn't help it.

"I'll stop, we don't have to finish baby, please don't cry." He said panicked.

"No!" I cried, my eyes springing open. "Don't stop, just give me a minute. Please, I don't want you to stop."

I reached up and kissed him hard, sucking his tongue into my mouth and biting his lips gently. Soon, the feeling inside changed and the pain flitted away leaving behind only yearning.

I didn't know what the feeling was but I knew that something had to change. I shifted slightly under him, forcing his cock to move just a bit inside me making waves of fire shoot out through me.

"Oh my God Lix, you have to do something, I need . . . something, please." I arched beneath him, unsure what I wanted or needed but the pressure was building inside me and I needed relief of some kind.

After another minute he pulled out of me and gently pushed back in. With every thrust the feelings got better and more intense and I thought I might explode. I might be a virgin but I wasn't completely naïve, I had masturbated before and made myself cum but this was different, better.

Lix's eyes were glued to my face and he continued his rhythm, pulling out and thrusting back in, only to speed up slightly. Then he pulled my leg around his waist and slid his hand between us and started rubbing my clit.

I thought I was going to rocket to the moon right then and as I started to cum again and my pussy muscles clenched around him he sped up faster and faster until he slammed into me one last time and held himself rigid, pushing his hips into mine though he hadn't pulled out.

Finally Lix collapsed on top of me, holding his weight on his arms panting. He kissed my cheek and my jaw, then my neck and my throat, sucking slightly on my pulse. He pulled back slightly to brush my hair off my forehead and kissed me there, too.

"I'm so sorry I hurt you baby, I didn't want to." He whispered, not looking at me. I tapped him on the shoulder and pushed slightly to get him to look at me so I could talk to him.

It's ok, I signed smiling slightly, *it had to be done and now it's over. And it was wonderful, thank you.*

He chuckled and shook his head, dropping his forehead to my chest. "You're welcome, I love you, you know." He kissed me on the lips before I could say anything and pulled out of me, stepping to the bathroom to take care of the condom.

When he came back he had a warm wash cloth that he placed between my legs, the heat soothing the ache. Finished with washing me he tossed the cloth into his hamper and snuggled in close to me.

"I got you a birthday present you know." He whispered in my ear.

I lunged up and turned to look at him with a frown.

"You took me out for supper, took me dancing, made love to me, what more is there? I've already had the best birthday."

He snorted and smiled, "I'm glad, but a pretty girl can't turn eighteen without a little something pretty to wear."

He reached over into the drawer of his nightstand and pulled out a small velvet box. Not a ring box, but slightly bigger and flatter. He handed it to me then put his hands behind his head and relaxed as I sat up, not caring about being naked in front of him.

I smiled at him and opened the box, not sure what I would find. Lying on the velvet inside was a silver box chain with a small butterfly hanging from it. The butterfly had small green peridots for the body and clusters of diamonds for its wings. It was absolutely beautiful and I loved it. I pulled it gently out of the box and held it out to him,

"Put it on me please," I asked, turning my back to him. He sat up and took the chain from me, placing the butterfly against my chest and clasping the chain behind my neck then lifting my hair from under it. I turned to him and smiled, leaning close to kiss him. "I love it, thank you. I love you, too."

Lix

I had tried so hard not to hurt Ashlyn and when she started to cry I felt like the worst boyfriend in the world. I knew the first time for her would hurt, had to hurt, but I still didn't like doing it. She was cuddled up with her head on my chest now playing with her necklace and every so often she would reach out and run her hand over my chest.

I held her tight, gently pulling her hair away from her face and letting it sift through my fingers. I had known before this that I loved her, but her giving herself to me cemented it. She was mine forever and that was all that mattered.

After that night Ashlyn stayed with me more often than not but she also started looking for an apartment of her own.

I thought that was great and when she asked me to go with her to find something we would both like I asked why that would matter.

You're going to be spending time there too aren't you? She signed, confused.

"Well, yeah but it's your place, it's more important that you like it." I said shrugging.

Of course, I'm not going to get a place if I don't like it but you do. She laughed and shook her head. *But I want you to be comfortable there.*

"Ok," I replied happily, "I can live with that." She took me to a really nice apartment building that I thought was going to cost a fortune.

I knew Needles paid her pretty decently but I thought this place would be out of her price range. When I asked her that she laughed and shook her head.

It's actually not bad, $1150 a month. She signed and shrugged. The building manager showed us into the place and let us look around. It was a really nice place, not huge but new and clean. She looked at me and I shrugged so she signed, *Be honest, do you like it?*

"Yeah," I said, "it's really nice and it sounds like it's affordable and it's safe."

"Uh, we don't have services for disabled people." The manager said apprehensively to Ashlyn. "I thought it would just be you living here?"

"Neither of us are disabled," Ashlyn said, shaking her head. "My boyfriend was injured in the armed forces and can't hear but he's not disabled."

"I can read your lips," I said to the man who had the grace to look sheepish.

"Sorry," He apologized, shaking his head, "I was rude, I apologize, I was just caught off guard."

"No problem," I shrugged, knowing this would be something we would have to deal with and that I had dealt with many times in the past.

I looked at Ashlyn to see how she was handling my disability being thrown in her face but she seemed to have moved on. It didn't seem to faze her at all as she was busy looking around the apartment again.

"I think I'll take it," she said, turning to the manager and smiling.

"Well ok then," the man said smiling, "Let's go down to the office and fill out the paperwork."

When the manager left I pulled Ash aside, "Are you sure about this place? We can keep looking."

"Oh no," She said, shaking her head. "I researched a few places in the last week and this one was the best option for the price. It's the safest and newest and it's close to everything. This place is even relatively close to work."

"Ok," I said nodding, "Let's go sign the paperwork then."

CHAPTER 8

Ashlyn

I loved my new apartment. It was small but not too small and I had a balcony that looked out onto a little courtyard. My dad had really wanted to buy me new furniture but I thought it would be easier if I just took my stuff from home.

We had three living rooms so I just picked out a few things and made Lix drag it over here for me. He was more than happy to help especially since I rewarded his hard work in my new bedroom.

Lix did spend more time here with me than he did at his room in the clubhouse which I also loved. That we could spend all that time together and not be interrupted or crowded by other people was so great. I felt so grown up having my own place, paying rent and buying groceries and cooking for myself and Lix.

Lix and I were having so much fun playing house, of course it wasn't playing since it was real life. My dad and step-mom came over for supper and so did Pixie and Seether and the guys from the MC and their wives or girlfriends all showed up at some point and we had a busy month getting settled and into a routine.

Technically Lix wasn't living at the apartment but he was over a lot. I finally told him to move his stuff over and just stay but I know he kept a lot of his stuff at the clubhouse still.

October was busy as well with Thanksgiving and Halloween and Lix's birthday. His mom and dad invited us down for Thanksgiving at their house in Kelowna, just over an hour south of Kamloops. I was so nervous and Lix just laughed at me as we drove. When we got to his parent's house I gaped at all the cars parked around the street.

"Who all is here?" I demanded frowning at Lix.

"Well, I told you I have three sisters," He replied shrugging. "Probably they came in one car each and their husbands probably came in another vehicle since they were out doing man stuff."

"Man stuff?"

"Yeah, my sisters married brothers, triplets actually." Lix said, smiling.

"Seriously?" I asked, he nodded and pulled me up to the front door. "There wasn't a sister for you to marry?"

"Oh, there's a sister, but there is no way in hell I am going to marry her, especially not now." He said, shaking his head.

"Why not now?" I asked, confused.

"Because now I have you to marry, I don't need my brothers-in-law setting me up with their annoying little sister." He shrugged and opened the front door, pulling me inside. "We're here!" he yelled and six little kids came running from the bowels of the huge house all screaming Uncle Lix!

A lovely looking older woman came out from what I figured was probably the kitchen wiping her hands on a towel then opened her arms wide to Lix. He wrapped his arms around her waist and held her close to him holding her up off the floor. When he finally put her down she cupped his face with her hands and smiled up at him with tears in her eyes.

"My boy," she said quietly. Lix just rolled his eyes at her and smiled indulgently.

"Mom, this is Ashlyn." He said holding his hand out to me. I put my hand in his and let him pull me to his side.

"Oh you're beautiful," Mrs. Taggart breathed and wrapped me up in a big hug that I really wasn't expecting.

"Marcy let the girl go!" boomed a voice from the right side of the entrance. I looked over to find four big men sitting in the living room watching hockey. Three of the men looked so much alike they had to be the triplet husbands. The other man was older and looked so much like Lix he could only be his dad.

"Mom, the potatoes are starting to boil over!" another feminine voice called from the left which when I turned to look I saw was a formal dining room.

"Oh!" Mrs. Taggart exclaimed and ran for the kitchen. Lix of course hadn't heard anything that had just happened and he probably wouldn't have noticed it if he had since he was too busy smiling at his mom hugging me.

"Sorry about that," A woman said coming from the dining room. She was a much younger version of Mrs. Taggart and looked to be about thirty, Bethie then, the oldest sister. "She's never met one of Lix's girlfriends before. I'm Bethie." She held out her hand and I shook it happily.

"Ashlyn," I replied smiling at Lix's sister.

"Lillian and Petra are in the kitchen with mom, you'll meet them later unless you'd rather go to the kitchen instead of watching hockey." Bethie said, smirking at her husband who was giving her a lustful look.

"Um, I'm not big into hockey, so the kitchen would be great."

"Follow me," Bethie laughed.

I found that all of Lix's sisters looked just like their mother. They were all rather tall, though not as tall as me, and all four women had golden blonde hair that fell in waves around their shoulders. The same colour hair that Lix had.

They all had the same blue eyes as him, too. Mrs. Taggart, who told me to call her Marcy was a busy woman who never stood still for more than five seconds before she was off starting something else.

Each of Lix's sisters had something about them that was special. Bethie was the oldest and had four kids. She was a romance novel writer and was quite famous under her pen name, I had even read some of her books and I loved them.

Lillian the middle sister had three kids and were registered dog breeders, a few of her dogs had actually been to the Westminster Kennel Club shows.

Petra the youngest sister had one kid and she was the artist. Many of her paintings were in galleries around the city and were displayed as far away as Ontario. One of her paintings had even sold for $500,000.

Lix always said he was the boring one in the family but I knew that wasn't true. He was the least boring person I knew. He was smart and funny and I loved him with all my heart. Mr. Taggart who insisted I call him dad was as tall as Lix, but bigger.

He had the barrel chested build of a man who had worked in heavy labour industries his whole life. He was much quieter than his wife who chattered to fill the silence but when Mr. Taggart had something to say everyone stopped talking to listen.

After everything was eaten and all the dishes were washed and put away and everyone was relaxing in the living room Mr. Taggart started talking.

"Ashlyn, I gotta tell you when our boy came back from Jordan he was not the same kid who left here." Mr. Taggart said and I knew that Lix wasn't paying attention to his dad so didn't know he was saying anything. "When Felix left here he was full of energy and always had a kind word and a quick laugh. When he came back he was a man who had seen too much and felt he had let everyone down, not just this family but the whole damn world because he was injured his first tour out."

"That's not true," I whispered sadly.

"We know that, but he's sitting there with you in his lap and he can't hear this conversation." Mr. Taggart replied, shaking his head. "When he came back he was so frustrated when we would talk around him, even when he went up to Kamloops to the MC he had a hard time with it. Now here he sits and we're not only talking around him but about him and he couldn't care less, and that's because of you. He's changed because of you, we saw it when we skyped with him, but now we see it even more and the change is not subtle."

When it was time for Lix and I to head home we hugged and talked with everyone in the entrance of the house for so long I was starting to think we wouldn't get out of there. Finally we were back in the truck and leaving the city limits behind.

"I know you guys were talking about me at the end there." Lix said not taking his eyes off the road. "It's ok, you don't have to say anything or explain. My parents forget I can mostly read lips and my dad talks so rarely I look for when his lips move."

They love you, I signed knowing he would see what I said out of the corner of his eye. And he did, and just nodded. *And so do I.*

He smiled at that and reached out a hand, cupping it around my thigh and pulling me across the truck to sit right next to him. The rest of the drive was in silence and when we got home to our little apartment he locked the front door and took me into the bedroom and made love to me so sweetly there was no doubt in my mind that he loved me, too.

Lix

Thanksgiving had been a lesson in patience for me. I had known my dad was talking to Ashlyn about me but I chose not to interrupt and wait to see what he said. He was right about it all. She had changed me.

Sure I was still cracking jokes and acting like my old self when I came back from the forces, but I didn't feel like the old me. Now, thanks to Ashlyn and the MC I felt like me and I felt like I didn't have the weight of the world crushing me into the ground.

Now it was Halloween and the women of the MC decided this would be a good night for a family dance to raise money for something or other. We were all expected to be at the clubhouse and help out. Ashlyn thought we should dress in matching costumes and I laughed at her.

"Why don't we both go as tough bikers," I said hoping she wouldn't push the subject. I was sadly disappointed because then she started talking to the other women and we all ended up dressing up as superhero couples.

Lo and Alana were Captain America and Peggy Carter, Axle and Brooke were Vision and the Scarlet Witch, Hammer and Kat were the Hulk and Black Widow, Seether and Pixie were Ant Man and Wasp. That left Ashlyn and I. She came home the afternoon of the party with two bags from the costume store and I really started to sweat.

It seemed we were sticking with the Marvel Universe so there were very few options left for couples. When she pulled out a black jumpsuit I started to get worried. That jumpsuit was far too big for her to wear and then she pulled out black dye hair spray and I wondered what she had planned until I saw the claws. I was Wolverine which meant she was either Storm or Jean Grey. I would be good with either but I nixed the jumpsuit.

"Wolverine wears jeans and wife beaters as often as he wears the jumpsuit, can't I just wear that?" I asked and I knew I was whining but I didn't care. Ashlyn dropped her hands to her sides and slumped her shoulders.

"Fine," She said disappointedly. I stepped to her and wrapped my arms around her waist, tipping my head to nibble on her neck.

"You can still do the hair and I'll still wear the claws," I murmured trailing kisses up her jaw and sucked her earlobe into my mouth. I knew she loved that and I would get my way and she would be happy. I felt her jaw move as she said something but of course I didn't catch it so I pulled back and looked at her. "What?"

She pushed away from me with a smirk and signed, *You seem to think you can get me to do anything. I signed you up to be DD to drive the drunks home.*

"Ah hell," I breathed putting my hands on my hips. "I guess this is my punishment for not wearing the stupid jump suit right?"

Yeah but I'll make it up to you later.

"How about you make it up to me now," I growled as I jumped at her grabbing her up in my arms and swinging her over my shoulder and rushing her into the bedroom, tossing her on the bed and following her down. "How much time do we have?"

Unfortunately not long enough, she giggled reaching up to kiss me. *I have to shower and you probably should, too.*

"Well then, let's conserve water and shower together." I pulled her up off the bed and into the bathroom. "Strip," I said as I turned and turned on the water, adjusting it to the right temperature. When I turned back to her she was naked and she slipped past me and into the tub.

As I watched her she tipped her head back under the spray and let the water wash over her hair. Ashlyn trailed her hands back over her hair, smoothing it and the extra water down her back, then trailed her hands over her breasts and down her stomach to her thighs.

She opened her eyes suddenly and looked directly into my eyes as she dipped her hands between her legs then up again to cup her breasts, plumping them and pinching her nipples. She smiled wickedly at me and bit her bottom lip then tipped her head back again, letting the water sluice over her head and body.

I don't think I had ever ripped my clothes off so fast before but within seconds I was in that tub with her and had her pinned against the wall, kissing her like I was starving in the desert.

Ashlyn kissed me back just as hungrily and lifted her leg to wrap around my waist. I cupped her ass and pulled her higher, letting my hard cock fit against her pussy. I thrust against her wetness but didn't enter her. She was wet but not wet enough and I didn't want to hurt her.

I left her mouth and trailed kisses down her throat and across her chest until I reached her breasts. I attached my mouth to her nipple and sucked hard, pulling her entire areola in. Her breasts were not large, maybe a C cup but they were perfect, high on her chest and full, her nipples the colour of raspberries and just as sweet to taste.

I dragged my tongue down her torso between her breasts to her belly button swirling my tongue into it then sucking on the skin just below it. I felt her breaths quicken as she started to pant and I sucked lower and lower on her belly until I hooked her leg over my shoulder and attacked her pussy with my mouth.

She arched into me and grabbed a fistful of my hair, holding me to her as I flicked my tongue over her clit then slid a finger into her wet heat. Her inner muscles clenched around my finger and I pulled it out and added another.

We had never talked about the back door, and I really didn't want that from her if she didn't want it but I knew that sometimes stimulation on the anal nerves could be very exciting. Anal sex didn't get me excited, but I wanted her to enjoy everything we did together.

As I sucked her clit into my mouth I spread her ass cheeks wide and rubbed my fingers over the cleft. With her clit in my mouth and two of my fingers in her pussy I knew she would come quickly anyway but I pushed a finger around and into her anus gently then pulled it away slightly.

I watched her face as I did this and I saw her eyes widen in surprise and then she was pushing her ass against my fingers, looking for more. Slowly and gently I pushed a finger all the way into her ass, pumping it in time with my fingers in her pussy.

Her entire body tensed and she pulled my hair, holding my mouth to her pussy as she rode my face until her orgasm was spent and she would have collapsed to my lap if I didn't hold her up.

I gently pulled my hands from her and rinsed my face in the water then stood up and kissed her deeply as I drove my cock into her. I pressed her into the wall and held her legs behind her knees, holding them around my waist and giving me leverage to thrust and hold her in place.

I knew that each thrust rubbed her already sensitive clit and I felt her shatter around me again as she bit into my shoulder, that little bit of pain sending me over the edge and I emptied my cum into her, twitching and shuddering until I too was spent.

Both of us were panting as I let her legs slowly lower to the floor of the tub but I held her up with my body, pressing her into the wall, knowing her legs were like rubber and might not hold her.

As she came down from her orgasms I kissed her deeply but gently, slipping my tongue into her mouth and licking the roof of her mouth until I felt her moan against my lips. Then I reached down to take care of the condom and stopped when I grabbed my dick.

"Shit!" I exclaimed looking down at my softening dick in my hand. Ashlyn tapped my shoulder so I would look at her. The question was clear on her face and she didn't need to take her hands from me to sign 'what?'. "Forgot the condom."

She watched my face for a second then started to laugh. *It's ok.*

"What if you get pregnant?" I demanded turning to the water and washing off then grabbing her shampoo to wash her hair for her.

I just finished my period; it's too soon for me to get pregnant.

"Are you sure?"

As sure as I can be without taking a test in two weeks. Ashlyn was obviously not worried about it so I decided not to worry about it either. I let out a sigh and kissed her then rinsed the shampoo from her hair. Then I finger combed her conditioner through her thick hair and moved her so I could wash my hair. She wasn't content to just watch though and couldn't seem to keep her hands from roaming all over my body.

"Keep that up and we're never going to make it to this party," I said with my head tipped back into the water, my eyes closed as I rinsed my hair. When I looked back at her she was smirking and her hands were cupping my ass.

"Now we have a problem, though." I said turning her so she could rinse the conditioner out of her hair. She raised her eyebrows in question. "Now that I've had you without a condom I don't want to go back to using them."

Ashlyn rolled her eyes and smiled then signed, *Me either, I'll look into ways to hold off pregnancy without birth control pills.*

"Excellent!" I exclaimed and kissed her before I turned off the water and we got out of the shower to get ready for the party. Fuck life was good.

CHAPTER 9

Lix

Two weeks after the party, which according to the women was a huge success and they had raised a ton of money, Ashlyn and I were standing in our apartment having an argument. Well, sort of. I know I was getting loud because every time I said something she cringed but she just kept shaking her head no. The look of determination on her face never changed.

It was really all my fault and I knew that but I still couldn't let it go. Two nights before I had mentioned wishing I could hear her voice, wondering if it was as beautiful as she was. I figured it had to be if it was hers.

That got her to thinking I guess and she started looking into cochlear implants. I had never bothered looking into it because I just didn't really care, I got by just fine without hearing and I didn't need to start hearing now.

I kept trying to tell her that but she was adamant. Ashlyn really wanted me to look into it. She had done some research online and thought I should talk to a specialist but that meant going to Vancouver which really was only a three hour drive but I just didn't want to do it.

Ashlyn had done some research and found that there was quite a bit of success with cochlear implants for patients with tinnitus like mine. Still, there was something holding me back and I just didn't know what it was. It was probably stupid but I just couldn't even talk about it.

Finally Ashlyn looked at me with a look that was pleading me to just think about it. I knew what she wanted to say but I couldn't hear it, or rather didn't want to hear it.

"No," I finally said, shaking my head then turned and left the apartment, letting the door slam behind me. I was angry but not at Ashlyn, I was angry at myself but I was still so confused.

Why didn't I want to even look into this? What was the big deal? Did I care that I was barely twenty and I would have hearing aids like an old man? No, that wasn't it but I just didn't know what it was.

I jumped in my truck and drove away, not sure where I would end up, I just drove. I knew Ashlyn was only trying to help, I knew she didn't care if I could hear or not. I also knew she wouldn't care if I wore hearing aids. Fuck I was messed up.

I ended up pulling my truck into the shooting range the MC used to keep our skills sharp. Not that we really needed it anymore but it was still a great way to relieve stress. I walked in and signed the forms and paid for my time and ammo then took the gun and headphones the guy behind the counter handed me. I walked down to the lane he pointed to and started shooting. I emptied three clips before I felt like I was calm enough to go home and talk to Ashlyn. So, I emptied another one before I got back in my truck and went home.

When I got to the apartment she was gone so I pulled out my phone and sent her a text.

I'm sorry, I'm home now and I'll wait for you
When you're ready to come home and talk
Like I should have stayed home before and talked

No rush, I can wait, just tell me you're safe. <3

Safe <3 be home soon

I knew she was still upset, otherwise she would have told me where she was and what she was doing, but I did get a heart back so she wasn't too mad. I would wait for her and when she got home I would prove to her how sorry I was for getting angry over something so stupid.

Ashlyn

When Lix slammed out of the apartment I stood in the middle of the living room in shock for about a minute. Then once I was sure his truck was gone and he wasn't coming back I grabbed my purse and my jacket and left as well. I jumped into my car and drove over to Pixie's house. I knew she and Seether were home because it was a Sunday; they never left the house on Sundays.

I pulled in behind Seether's giant truck and Pixie's new SUV that he had bought her when she had gotten pregnant. He said his truck was too big for her to drive and try to climb into with a baby belly. She shook her head and rolled her eyes but really Seether had more money than the Prime Minister so what did it matter.

I walked up to their front door but couldn't make myself knock so I sat on the swing on the porch. It didn't take long before Pixie stepped out and sat beside me.

"What are you doing out here?" I demanded after a couple of minutes. "You're not even wearing a coat."

"This baby keeps me plenty warm," she smirked, rubbing her belly. She was about six months along but still not showing very much. She said it was because she had been so thin before she got pregnant and she was tall so the baby had lots of room to stretch out. I didn't know how true that was but she would know better than I would. "So, what did Lix do?"

"Nothing," I muttered on a sigh.

"Oh come on, I'm also a woman, I know that nothing really means something."

"No, I mean he did nothing, he won't do anything. He said he wished he could hear my voice so I looked into ways that he could get his hearing back. Cochlear implants are really very successful for patients like him but he refused to even consider it."

"Oh sweetie," Pixie said, wrapping her arm around my shoulder. "Does it really matter?"

"No of course not, if Lix never hears again and he's ok with that then fine, I'm not going to argue about it. What I'm arguing about is that he's not even going to consider it. At some point if we stay together, and it looks like we will, we might have kids and he's going to want to hear them." I shook my head looking out at the street that ran in front of Pixie's house. "I just want him to consider it."

"Come on," Pixie said standing beside me and pulling on my hand. "Aiden started making lunch when he saw you pull up. I'm pretty sure he's making your favourite."

"Ice cream sundaes?" I asked looking up at her hopefully. She smirked and nodded. "Let's go then."

I was just finished my ice cream and asking Seether for his advice when Lix texted me. I had been laughing with my sister and Seether but as soon as I saw his message the hurt came back. I sent him a quick message telling him I would be home soon and I was safe then started eating my ice cream again but much more slowly. When Pixie got tired of hearing my spoon hit my very empty dish every time I tried to get more ice cream she took my bowl away.

"Come on, Ash. Time to go home," She held out my jacket with a smile and I nodded letting her help me into it. I hugged her and

Seether and left their house for the quick drive home. When I got there Lix was sitting on the couch staring at a black TV. He looked up when he caught motion out of the former of his eye and jumped to his feet.

"I'm sorry," He said, stepping towards me. "I shouldn't have gotten mad, I shouldn't have gotten upset, you were only trying to help, I know that."

Why won't you even consider it? I signed tipping my head to the side.

"I don't know," he replied, shoving his hands into his pockets. "I really don't. I thought about it the whole time I was out and I can't come up with a reason."

Are you afraid of the surgery?

He screwed up his face, thinking about it but then shook his head no. "I don't think so, I'm not afraid of pain or anything like that."

Are you afraid that you'll go through it all and it won't work?

"Maybe," he shrugged but didn't seem convinced. "Look, I'll look at the stuff you found but not today. Please let me show you how sorry I am."

I shook my head looking at him and sighed, *You don't have to show me anything. I know you're sorry, doing anything now would be to settle your own conscience.*

"That's true," He said nodding and looked down at his feet. "Did you eat? Do you want to get something to eat?"

I shook my head no. I really was still full from the ice cream.

"Can I run you a bath?"

Will you get in with me?

"If that's what you want then absolutely!" he said smiling and rushing forwards, gathering me up into his arms and holding me tightly. "I love you, so so much."

"I love you, too." I said behind his back, "I just wish you could hear me say it like this."

He pulled back and looked into my eyes. "Did you say something?" But I shook my head no and smiled.

CHAPTER 10

Ashlyn

For the last week everything went back to normal. Lix did look at the cochlear implant information and seemed to be thinking about it but hadn't brought it up again. That was fine. He was considering it at least.

We were the last two at the tattoo parlor and we were just about to lock up. He had put away all the tools he and the other guys used and cleaned everyone's stations. I was counting the till and then I would help with the sweeping and mopping.

We hadn't had any business for at least an hour so we were able to get everything done pretty quickly. When it was all finished he locked the back door and I waited for him at the front then we both stepped out together onto the sidewalk and I waited again as he locked the front.

Before I knew what was happening the glass of the front window had shattered causing the alarm to go off. It sounded extra loud in the quiet night and as I turned to Lix he grunted and fell to the ground. I screamed as the tires of a car peeled away down the street and then I was on my knees beside Lix.

He was at least still breathing but completely unconscious. November at night was not the best time to be out in the middle of the street with an unconscious man. I pulled out my phone and called 911 and was assured that police and EMTs were on their way. Then I pulled out Lix's phone and called Needles.

"Hello?" Needles' voice came through the speaker.

"Needles? It's me Ash, are you busy right now? Can you come down to the shop?" I asked knowing I was losing what little calm I had.

"Uh yeah I'm just waiting on a tow truck, then we'll catch a cab right over. What's wrong?"

"Um, well Lix and I were just leaving the shop and locking up when a car drove past and threw a brick through the window." I said and my voice starting to get shrill.

"Did you call the police?"

"Yeah, but that's not it." I replied as I started to sob. "There were two bricks thrown, one went through the window and the other hit Lix in the head. He's unconscious. I called 911 on my phone and then took his out of his pocket and called you. I'm sitting out in front of the shop alone with an unconscious man lying across my lap and it's getting dark and it's cold and I'm really scared."

"Ok, Ash just hang on, I'll send out a message and see if any of the other guys are in the area and can meet you there and stay with you. Don't worry, someone will be there soon. Siobhan and I are getting a cab now and we'll be there ASAP, ok?"

"Ok Needles, I'll wait,"

"Are you still on the line with the 911 operator?" He asked.

"Yeah, she's talking to someone else now but she's still there." I replied, sniffing. "Oh, Casey just came on the line . . .

"Hey sweetheart," Casey said into my ear, "You doin' alright?"

"Yeah I'm ok . . ."

"Listen the police should be right around the corner from you now."

"Yeah I can hear the sirens now . . . "

"Ok sweetheart, don't you worry. The EMTs are going to take care of Lix for you ok and the police will take care of you ok?"

"Thanks Casey. Needles?"

"Yeah Ash, I'm still here." An ambulance and a police car stopped at the curb in front of me and four people jumped out, rushing around.

"Miss, are you ok?" One of the Constables asked.

"I'm fine, my boyfriend is hurt, though." I replied not letting go of the phone and the connection to Needles.

"Ok Miss, do either of you work at this establishment?"

"Yes, we both do, I'm on the phone now with the owner." I replied sniffing again.

"Is the owner coming here now?" the Constable asked crouching beside me.

"The ambulance and the police are here now; they just pulled up in front of the shop. I gotta go, the police want to know if you're coming here or going to the hospital first?"

"Tell them I'll meet you all at the hospital ok? You be strong for Lix ok Ash?"

"Ok Needles, see you soon?"

"Yeah sweetheart, we'll see you soon. I'll call Pixie too and get her to call your dad ok?"

"Thanks Needles see you soon," I hung up and looked up at the EMTs who were pulling the stretcher out of the back of the ambulance. The policeman was still crouched beside me trying to get my attention but I wasn't ready to pay attention to him yet. I took a deep breath as the EMTs rushed to me and lifted Lix's head so I could move from underneath him.

"Miss?" The Constable said touching my elbow.

"Sorry, the owner is going to meet us at the hospital." I replied not taking my eyes off of Lix.

"Miss," one of the EMTs said, getting my attention. "Can you tell us the victim's name and age? Does he have any allergies we need to know about?"

"His name is Felix Taggart," I said moving quickly closer to Lix's side. "He's twenty, almost twenty-one. He has no allergies that I know of but he is deaf, he suffered a brain injury that caused him to lose his hearing."

"Ok miss, will you be riding in the ambulance with Mr. Taggart?"

"Yes please."

Lix

I was sitting in Pixie and Seether's living room and I didn't know why. Seether was in his office doing whatever it was that Seether did and Pixie and Ashlyn were running around setting up a bedroom for me.

"Does someone want to tell me what the hell is going on?" I demanded loudly I'm sure. No one came running to talk to me so I slowly got up from the couch and once I wasn't so dizzy I walked into Seether's office. "What the hell man? Why aren't I going home?"

Seether said something but he never once took his eyes off his monitor so I didn't catch any of it.

"Hey man, I didn't catch that." Instead of answering this time he held up a finger for me to wait so I sat in the other office chair positioned in front of yet another computer. This place was full of computers. Worse I heard than Seether's room at the clubhouse had been. Especially now with Pixie's stuff set up it was hacker heaven. Sitting in the chair next to Seether's I tipped my head back and closed my eyes until I felt a tap on my knee. I sat up and looked at Seether.

Ash's dad doesn't know you live with her, that's why you're here. Pixie thought Ash was too shook up over what happened to have that conversation with her dad in the hospital. Seether signed, then suddenly looked over at the door of the room. I followed his gaze much slower to find Ashlyn there looking sheepish. I stood slowly and walked over to her.

"You didn't tell your dad about us?" I asked her quietly, I think.

He knows we're together, he just doesn't know you're living with me. She signed and I watched her lips move so I know she was saying everything she signed.

"Why didn't you tell him?"

I don't know. She signed and then shrugged. *Scared I guess. I'm sorry.*

"Ok," I said, taking her in my arms. "Can we go home now?"

She shook her head no and pulled away from me. *Tomorrow, I need Seether's help if anything goes wrong with your concussion.*

"Ok," I said again then asked her to take me up to the room they had gotten ready for me. "Are you staying here with me?" She nodded yes so I let her lead me up the stairs and help me get into bed. It was pretty late at night, close to midnight actually so I knew she was exhausted. She set her phone alarm to go off every two hours to wake me up.

"I love you," I said holding her close, "Thank you for taking care of me." She smiled up at me so I kissed her lips then tucked her head under my chin and went to sleep.

It was a week later when it all went to shit.

Needles had closed the shop for a week as he worked on getting the window fixed and the shop back together. Ashlyn and I didn't go in to work that whole week and the day after the brick incident we moved back to our apartment.

Her dad stopped by a couple of times and she sat him down and told him I was living there. It went a long way to soothing my anger that she hadn't told him in the first place.

Mr. Cameron just looked at me and told me to take care of his little girl or he'd kill me. I nodded, completely understanding what he was saying. He may not actually kill me but he had ways to make me wish I was dead. I respected that.

Once again, late at night Ash and I were leaving the shop. We had been in with Needles and Siobhan finishing the final set up for our grand re-opening the next day. Ash and I were standing on the sidewalk locking up when I realized I had forgotten my cell phone.

"Shit," I said, pulling the door open. "I forgot my phone, I'll be right back."

I didn't wait to see if she said anything which was stupid but I figured I'd be half a second and then back to her. Except when I got back to the door she was gone.

"Ash?" I called, "Where are you baby?" I shrugged and figured she'd gone to the truck because she was cold so I locked up and headed to the truck.

I locked up and headed out to the parking lot, wanting to get home soon and get her into bed and make love to her.

CHAPTER 11

Ashlyn

"Shit! I forgot my phone, I'll be right back." Lix said and disappeared back into the store.

"Hurry up," I called knowing he wouldn't hear me anyway. "It's freaking cold out here!" I turned away from the store to watch the street and I was just about to turn back when I felt a pinch in my side through my jacket.

"Let's go," A voice rasped in my ear.

"What? No –"

"Oh yes little Ashlyn, we're going far from here and you're going to give me what I want." The man said; his grip on my elbow bruising.

"No, my boyfriend –"

"Won't hear you screaming," the man laughed as I struggled. He was far too strong for me to get away from him, though. "Stop fighting me!" He exclaimed and drew back a fist and punched me in the stomach. I grunted at the pain and doubled over, holding my midsection as I gasped for air.

"I won't need this yet," He said, holding up a small knife in front of my face then put it in his pocket and grabbed a handful of my hair, pulling me to stand upright. "Come on little girl, you're mine now."

I heard myself whimper as he dragged me to the alley and shoved me down the wide space full of garbage.

The shop had a back door that opened onto this alley and I knew it had a camera above it that spanned the entire space.

My only hope was to get there, then even if Lix didn't make it out here to help me I would have this guy's face on camera.

I pulled away from him and ran to the door, throwing myself against it and banging on it. I knew it was locked from the inside and I knew Lix wouldn't hear me banging but this guy didn't know we weren't alone, right?

"I'm going to take what I want from you little girl." The man said snidely, his lip curling in disgust. "I guess if I can't have Siobhan I'm going to have to have you."

That's when I really looked at him and realized who he was.

"Mr. Zane, please don't do this," I begged but it just made him angrier.

He lashed out with a fist and punched me across the face, splitting the skin above my cheekbone. I fell to my knees on the filthy ground starting to sob then I started to scream. Lix couldn't hear me but someone else must be able to.

"Shut the fuck up!" Zane screamed pulling my hair and dragging me back to get right in my face.

Then he let go of my hair and started to punch me and kick me over and over again but I didn't stop screaming. I screamed so much my voice grew hoarse and I finally couldn't scream anymore.

Now I just whimpered and begged him to stop, tears running down my cheeks, the salt stinging the cut on my cheek.

"Now that you're quiet I'm going to have you like I want you," Zane smirked, reaching for his belt buckle with one hand while the other started pulling at my leggings.

"No," I cried, starting to kick and getting a second wind, knowing what his plan now was and knowing I couldn't live through that.

Just as Zane knelt in front of me, shoving my legs wide a roar filled the alley so loud I thought my ear drums would shatter and then Zane was gone and the alley was full of the grunts of men fighting.

Lix

Where the hell did she go? Ash wasn't on the sidewalk, she wasn't in the truck and all the stores around us were closed. Did she go back into the shop? No, I would have seen her, so where the hell was she? Finally I started walking up and down the street. I went to the corner and turned down it, going a little ways but snow was starting to fall and there were no footprints except mine.

I turned and went back the way I came and went across the front of the store to the alley beside the shop. When I got to the corner of the building I saw a movement deep by the store's back door. I rushed down there thinking maybe Ash had gotten hurt or was looking for something. What I found there made my blood run cold and then super-heated.

A man had Ash on the ground and had been beating her. He was now pulling her pants off, trying to rape her. I lost my mind. I let out a yell that felt loud but for all I knew it was silent in the deafening roar in my ears.

I reached out and grabbed the man by the collar of his jacket and yanked him away from Ash, throwing him against the wall. I looked at her just long enough to get sucker punched in the face then I turned to him and started whaling on him. I didn't care where I hit him; I didn't care if I killed him. He had hurt Ash and that was all that mattered.

At some point he had lost the ability to stand and I was holding him up as I punched him. Then the blood cleared from my eyes and I looked down at a tug on the leg of my jeans. Ash had crawled over to us and was trying to get my attention. I let go of the guy and knelt beside her, picking her up in my arms and carrying her out of the alley.

She was trying to say something but I couldn't read her lips with them swollen and split.

"Sh baby, it's ok, I've got you," I said trying to soothe her. She shook her head slightly and held up her phone. I saw the screen read 911 and she tilted her head to the side listening. The police must be on their way. I sat on the edge of the sidewalk holding her until a cop car skidded to a stop in front of us.

Ashlyn tapped my shoulder and pointed to the cop standing in front of me but I just shook my head. I wasn't talking to anyone; I was only going to hold Ashlyn until they made me give her up. Soon the EMTs were taking her from me and I was following them to the ambulance when something caught their attention and they all turned to the alley.

Before I knew it one of the EMTs were running back to the alley as the other was getting Ashlyn ready for transport. I was just about to climb in the back with her when my arm was grabbed and a cop pulled me back, putting handcuffs on my wrists, dragging me away from her.

I started fighting, I had no idea what was going on and I could see Ashlyn getting upset in the back of the ambulance, trying to sit up but the EMT with her kept her down and eventually gave her a needle of something.

My girl was hurt and upset and I was being shoved into the back of a police car.

"Hey!" I yelled at the cops in the front seat. "Hey, I can't hear you! I'm deaf, what the hell is going on? Do either of you know sign language? Seriously you guys, please my girl was hurt I gotta go to the hospital."

The only thing these two cops did was laugh while one of them flipped me the bird. I was well and truly screwed.

It was hours later, after I had been processed and fingerprinted, questioned and then thrown in a cell that someone actually came to talk to me. The cop that had questioned me said the guy I beat up was Dean Zane, a high profile lawyer in town. I still hadn't convinced these guys that I couldn't hear a word they said but what I read from their lips didn't give me much hope.

Finally Sharpie, the club lawyer, showed up. I was taken to meet him in an interrogation room and left with him.

"Fuck Sharpie, what the hell is going on?" I demanded, sitting at the table across from him. "Is Ashlyn ok? What the hell happened? Who the hell is Dean Zane and why did he attack Ash?"

Dean Zane is the ass wipe that's been harassing Siobhan. Sharpie signed sighing heavily. *We don't know yet why he attached Ashlyn; we only know that he's pressing charges against you for beating his ass up.*

"I was protecting Ash, check the camera!" I yelled; standing and shoving my chair back.

I know, Sharpie signed holding his hands out for me to calm down. *Until Seether gets the video from the shop you're stuck in here. Either way as far as I know Ashlyn is ok, she's beat up but he didn't rape her. She'll be in the hospital for a couple of days so they can make sure there's no internal bleeding but after that she's free to go home.*

"I didn't protect her Sharpie," I said suddenly, slumping back into my chair. "I couldn't hear her screaming; I couldn't protect her."

I put my elbows on my knees and buried my face in my hands and cried.

Sharpie sat with me for another half an hour or so as I told him what had happened, at least what I knew and then he promised he would be back tomorrow with the video that exonerated me and put Zane in jail.

He also told the cops that yes I was deaf and they had better treat me a whole lot better or he would be filing charges against the detachment for miss-treatment.

This was going to be the longest night of my life, or so I thought.

CHAPTER 12

Ashlyn

"Knock knock," I looked up to see Siobhan in the curtained door-way of the little room I was in, then ducked her head inside the curtain and saw me lying on a bed with tears streaming down my cheeks. "Constable MacDonald, I just need to ask the patient some questions." she said flashing her badge.

"Sure," the doctor said nodding, "I'm almost finished here. I sure hope you get the guy who did this, he was quite brutal."

"Hey Ash," Siobhan said quietly, pulling a stool close to the bed.

"Siobhan?" I asked weakly, my voice raspy from being strangled.

"Yeah sweetie, can you tell me who did this to you?"

"I don't know his name." I cried, I could feel my tears flowing faster now.

"Can you describe him to me?"

"He was tall, but not as tall as Seether, like Lix and Needles. He had dark hair and I guess he was handsome, some people might think so I guess. He smelled like cologne and he wore a suit. No Siobhan, I did know him, I recognized him, I said his name but I can't remember it now."

"Ok sweetie, I'm going to show you a couple of pictures, can you tell me if you recognize anyone?" I nodded as she pulled her phone out of her pocket. Siobhan flipped through a few other photos of guys and girls from the MC and came to the one of Dean. I grabbed her casted wrist, and gripped her tightly.

"That's him! Siobhan, that's the guy." I sobbed pointing at her phone.

"Ok Ash, I'm going to go and get your dad and Pixie ok, you just relax here and I'll send them in ok."

"Siobhan where's Lix, is he here? Can he come in, too?"

"I'll look for him ok," she said and then was gone.

A few minutes later Pixie came in with my dad. They were both crying. I had only seen my dad cry once before and that was when Pixie came back into our lives about a year ago. He hadn't even cried when mom had died, he'd been upset yes but he hadn't cried. Now he stood in the entrance of the room looking at me with tears running down his cheeks and he looked twenty years older than his age.

"Daddy?" I whispered, watching him crumple right in front of me. He stepped across the room and sat in the chair Siobhan had just vacated, taking my hand in his, kissing it and holding it to his wet cheek. Pixie walked around the other side of the bed and took my other hand, smoothing my hair back from my forehead.

"Hey sweetie," She said smiling down at me. "I talked to the doctor; he says you have a couple of broken ribs and a concussion, a few stitches. They're going to keep you here for a few nights to make sure there's no internal bleeding, ok?"

"No," I cried, shaking my head, "I want to go home, I want Lix, where's Lix?"

"Hey, it's ok," Pixie said calmly, "It's just a few nights and I'll be here the whole time, I promise."

"No, you need your rest for the baby, you have to go home, send Lix here." I said more adamantly than before.

"I can't sweetie, he was arrested." Pixie finally said, shocking me.

"But he didn't do anything wrong," I exclaimed then coughed when my throat complained.

"We know but he beat up the guy who did this to you, almost killed him and the guy is pressing charges." Dad explained, trying to keep me calm, it wasn't working.

"Aiden is working on getting the video from the camera at the back of the shop to prove that Lix was protecting you. Sharpie is already talking with Lix and getting this all straightened out. Siobhan just went and arrested Zane, cuffed him to his hospital bed." Pixie said, smirking at that last part.

"Ok, but you make sure Lix comes to me as soon as he gets out of jail. You tell him I need him." I demanded as a nurse and an orderly came in to move me to a private room.

"Of course sweetie," Pixie promised, following me out of the room. "As soon as I can get him here I will."

***

Lix didn't come to the hospital, though. I was there for a total of three nights and he never came. I knew he was out of jail because Pixie and Aiden told me he was but they couldn't explain why he wasn't coming to visit.

I thought maybe he would come and get me when I was released from the hospital, but he still didn't show up. I had planned on going straight home but Pixie had brought me an envelope she had found on my kitchen counter.

When I opened it a key fell out and a single piece of paper that just read 'I'm sorry' in Lix's handwriting. Pixie said all of his things were gone so she packed some clothes for me so I could stay at my dad's.

I had my phone back and I sent Lix a text asking him where he was and what was going on but I didn't get an answer, not even a heart or an emoji or anything. I was so confused that he wouldn't even talk to me, I didn't know what to do.

For the entire month that I stayed with my dad I sent Lix a text every day.

Where are you?

No answer . . .

Why won't you talk to me?

No answer . . . I even resorted to begging,

Please answer me, I miss you Lix, please talk to me.

Still no answer. Finally after a month of being pampered at my dad's house I moved back to my apartment. Everything there reminded me so much of Lix but at the same time it was so devoid of everything that was him.

I spent Christmas with my dad and step-mom and Pixie and Seether came over, too. We all had a great time except for this feeling of loss that kept following me around.

Later that night I got a text from Lix's sister Bethie.

**Merry Christmas, we heard about what happened,
Lix is here and physically ok.**

> **OMG, thank you for texting me Bethie!
> He won't talk to me, he won't come and see me,
> I don't know what to do!**

**I wish I could say give it time, but I don't know
What will help. We're all praying that he comes
To his senses.**

> **Do you know why he's cut me off? Why**
> **He won't talk to me?**

He talked to dad about it but dad just shakes his
Head when we ask about it.

Lix is really torn up about it and I think he blames
Himself.

> **What? What could he possibly blame himself for?**

Because he didn't get to you soon enough.

I was too shocked to answer that. I just stared at the message and let my tears flow. My Lix blamed himself for me being hurt and there was nothing further from the truth. The next text that came through had me pushing away my tears.

Anyway, we all just wanted to say Merry Christmas,
And we're glad you're doing better. Don't give up
On him Ash, please? He's hurting right now and confused.

> **Merry Christmas to all of you, too Beth,**
> **Thanks for texting me, I'll try.**
> **Give everyone there hugs for me.**

He was hurting? I could understand that really, because I was hurting, too! I was mad for all of two minutes before it all came crashing down and I collapsed on my bed and cried myself to sleep.

When I woke up the next morning I knew I had to go out to the clubhouse to talk to him. I knew he wasn't there right now because he was at his parents but as soon as he was back I was going out there. I had also decided I wasn't going to be a victim ever again. I decided I was going to start taking self defense classes and going to the gym. I was never going to be weak again.

CHAPTER 13

Lix

It had been a month since Ash had been attacked and I had been arrested. She kept sending me texts and I kept reading them then ignoring them. They were all saved on my phone because I refused to delete them but I couldn't answer them. I was no good for her. I couldn't protect her and I couldn't ever be enough for her.

I was sitting now on my parents back porch with a beer in my hand. I was twenty-one and I felt like I had lost everything that ever mattered. I should have been spending today with Ashlyn, our first Christmas. I still had her gift.

I had gotten her a few little things that I knew she would like but I had gotten her one big thing that I knew would blow her away. She had loved the butterfly pendant I had gotten her for her birthday and I had found a bracelet that matched it perfectly. It was sitting in my room at the clubhouse right now.

I didn't know what to do with it. Should I take it back to the store? No, I really couldn't do that, I couldn't force myself to. Should I send it to her? Maybe but was that really fair to her?

What the fuck was I thinking; none of this was fair to her. I was taking a sip of my beer when my dad came out and sat beside me.

I felt him sigh and then he turned his chair so his back was to the yard and he was facing me so I could see his hands.

What's going on, son?

"Nothin' dad, it's just done." I said, shrugging drinking more beer.

Bull shit.

"Yeah, it is but that's all I got."

Tell me, no one else here but you and me.

"It's my fault she was hurt." I said after a minute. I refused to make eye contact but I could still see dad's hands when he signed.

More bull shit.

"That it is not, it's the truth. I shouldn't have left her standing on that sidewalk, I should have been able to hear her screaming, I should have known she was in that alley and not walked the other direction or out to the truck."

You think that because you can't hear she got hurt?

"I know that if I could hear she wouldn't have been hurt as bad and I know that if I wasn't so fucking stupid she wouldn't have been hurt at all."

All the blame for this lies at the feet of that Zane, none of this is on you.

"Doesn't matter now," I said finishing my beer. "It's done."

No son, I don't think it is and I hope you see that sooner rather than later before it really is done. My dad stood, clapping me on the shoulder and walked back into the house. I didn't follow him for a long time, pulling another bottle of beer from the box beside me and finishing it before I went in the house.

By the time I got there all the lights were off and my parents were in bed. Just as I was about to slide under the sheets of my child-hood bed my phone vibrated with an incoming message.

Merry Christmas Lix, I love you, I don't blame you, please answer me.

Ashlyn, it was almost like she had been on that porch with my dad and me. But it was too late. I shut off my phone without answering her and lay down on the bed and stared at the ceiling until the sun started to peak over the horizon.

***

I had been back at the clubhouse for a week when there was a knock on the door of my room. I of course didn't hear it but the pounding that came after certainly got my attention. I cursed and walked over, opening it wide planning on yelling at whoever was there to bother me.

Lo stood there and I knew my plans to get mad would have to wait but then he turned and walked away and Ashlyn was standing in the hallway.

"Fuck!" I exclaimed and turned my back on her. She couldn't talk to me if I didn't look at her. She walked into the room and stopped in front of me, then walked until she backed me against the wall and I couldn't turn away from her.

Stop this please, come home. She signed and tears were cascading down her cheeks but I couldn't look at her face. I shook my head no and crossed my arms over my chest to keep me from taking her in my arms. *Please Lix, I need you.*

"No, you need someone who can take care of you, who can protect you, that's not me." I said, shaking my head still refusing to look at her.

She sighed heavily then signed *You're wrong, I hope you figure that out before you're too late.* Then she stepped up to me, stretching onto her toes and kissed my cheek and was gone. As the door latched closed I took a deep breath of the scent she left behind and let the tears flow down my own cheeks.

I stayed against the wall and slid down until my ass touched the floor, completely unable to control my sobs as in my heart I said goodbye to the only person I would ever love.

A month later nothing had changed. The charges against me were dropped almost as soon as I was released from jail the morning after Ashlyn was attacked. Zane was still in jail and waiting for his own trial but I didn't care. I had nothing to do with that.

I worked at the tattoo parlor and came home to the clubhouse and slept poorly in my own bed. Ashlyn had gone back to working with her dad instead of coming back to the parlor and I couldn't blame her.

I doubted she was avoiding me because she still texted me every day, often having one sided conversations about her day and what she did or the people she met at her dad's office. That was the highlight of my dad, lying in bed wishing she was beside me. I knew though that was impossible.

It was the end of January and I was at loose ends. Nothing was enough to keep me going anymore. I would go to work and I couldn't concentrate so I would grab a sketch pad to draw and I would find those first notes Ash wrote me.

I would think about throwing them out but I couldn't do it so I'd flip the page and start drawing and by the time I was done it was her face staring back at me, only it was never as simple as that.

I would always draw her sleeping, or just as she was climaxing with an orgasm, or how she looked at me over her shoulder when I was doing her tattoo. One was even how she looked with her head tipped back in the shower, water sluicing through her hair and down her naked body.

The worst one, though that I couldn't get out of my head no matter how many times I drew it was how she looked that day in my room when she begged me to come back to her. Fuck I was losing my mind.

It was about that time that I was sitting in the kitchen eating something bland and tasteless. I was alone for the most part as just about everybody avoided me like the plague now. Not that I blamed them, I was always angry.

Nick, who we called Saint, sat beside me but I ignored him. That is I ignored him until he reached over and slapped the back of my head.

"What the fuck, asshole!" I yelled, jerking back away from him.

When are you going to pull your head out of your ass?

"Fuck you," I muttered and went back to eating. Out of the corner of my eye I saw him raise his hand again but I caught his wrist before he could actually hit me. He narrowed his eyes at me until I let go of his hand.

Ashlyn needs you.

"She does fucking not!" I went back to eating and Nick knocked on the table just under my line of sight. I ignored him, done with any conversation but he only knocked harder. In fact he was knocking hard enough to rattle the dishes. Finally I must have really pissed him off because he slammed his hand on the table and swiped my plate away from me and onto the floor.

"Fuck off!" I yelled at him jumping out of my chair. "She doesn't fucking need me! She's better off without me!"

You're so fucking stupid! Nick signed and I could tell he was yelling at me at the same time. *Whether she needs you or not she wants you! I would kill for that and you've got it and you're throwing it away! You fucking idiot!*

Nick shoved me and stormed out of the kitchen. I stood with my hands on my hips breathing hard and seething when Brooke came in. Her steps were slow and pensive like she was afraid I was going to blow up at her, too.

"I'm not going to hurt you," I sighed, rubbing a hand over my face then over my head, pushing my hair back.

I know. She signed and smiled slightly but sadly. *Nick is right you know.*

"So what if he is? Doesn't change anything." I replied shrugging.

Siobhan set Ash up with her brother you know. Lachlan told me about it the other day.

I didn't say anything because I knew Brooke was trying to get a rise out of me.

You know, I talked to Alana about Drew's cochlear implants. She says they're amazing and help him a lot. I shrugged at her sure she was making a point. *Ashlyn mentioned talking to you about them, from what she said you could actually hear with them.*

"What's your point?" I demanded glaring at her.

No point, just wondering why you're not doing it.

Suddenly I was wondering the same thing. But that wouldn't change the past. I turned and left the kitchen and Brooke behind, storming to my room. I stripped out of my jeans and put on a pair of athletic shorts and went to the gym we had in the clubhouse to work out. I needed some way to get this extra adrenaline out of my system and think.

Did I want to even consider the implants? And really, why the hell wouldn't I? What the hell was holding me back? Was Ashlyn right and I was just scared? I hadn't lied to her, I wasn't afraid of pain but was I afraid that it wouldn't work after all and I would still be stuck with the ringing?

Fuck, I needed to do some research of my own and talk to my doctor. But first I needed to figure some other shit out, like how the hell to get Lachlan away from Ashlyn.

CHAPTER 14

Ashlyn

Pixie and Siobhan were playing matchmaker, the little sneaks. They had set up a group date with them and their men and me and Lachlan, Siobhan's brother. He was a year older than me and really a very sweet guy. He chatted with me through dinner and we had a very good time.

By the time dinner was over Pixie was super tired and wanted to go home to bed, she only had another three weeks of her pregnancy to go and she was always tired now. The six of us said good-bye and I got into Pixie's SUV.

"Well," she demanded as soon as the doors were closed. "Do you like him?"

"Pix," Seether warned quietly, taking her hand.

"What? Lachy's a nice guy."

"You know he hates being called that right?" I said to her referring to the nickname his sister called him. "He prefers to be called Lachlan."

"Oh, so you did actually talk to him." Pixie said turning in her seat to look at me.

"Stop Pixie, he's a nice guy but I'm not making any promises." I said as Seether pulled the car in front of my apartment.

"Fine," Pixie said, rolling her eyes. "Hurry inside; we'll wait until you get in the door."

"Are you ok to go in alone?" Seether asked, turning in the seat to look at me.

"I'll be fine, thanks. Take my sister home and put her to bed, she's falling asleep." I said smiling at them both. "I'll talk to you guys later."

We all said goodnight and I rushed inside the glass door at the front of the building. Once it was closed I looked back and waved then Seether drove away. I hurried up to my apartment and let myself in then locked the door. I decided a long hot bath was just what I needed so I started the water as I checked the doors and windows to make sure they were all locked.

As I waited for the tub to fill my phone chimed with an incoming text. I grabbed it quickly thinking, and hoping, it was Lix but it wasn't, it was Lachlan. I smiled thinking about him, even though he wasn't the one I wanted to hear from.

I had a good time tonight Ashlyn, thanks for supper

Me too Lachlan

**I don't suppose you want to do it again without
The chaperones?**

Oh, uh sure, that actually sounds fun

**There's a few new releases tomorrow, do you
Want to go to the movies? Maybe grab a bite to
Eat first?**

Yeah, that sounds like a great idea

Cool, I'll pick you up at 5?

Absolutely, I'll see you then!

I couldn't believe it. I had just made a date with a great guy who wasn't Lix. I really didn't want anyone but Lix right now but he obviously didn't want me so maybe I should move on, and why not? Well, probably because I still loved Felix Taggart, but I would just have to get over it.

I decided what I needed right now was not a bath but a long run on the treadmill in the building's gym and maybe some weight training. My body had changed in the month that I had been working out.

My arms had definition and my stomach was no longer soft but ridged with muscle. I was also stronger and faster. My trainer and my self defense coach had both said so. I felt good, too but no safer. I was good at faking it though.

When I had run as much as I could and my arms and legs were tired from the weights I made my way back to my apartment and finished running the bath I had started earlier, sinking into the hot water and letting it soothe my tired muscles and my sort heart.

The next afternoon, Lachlan showed up at my apartment building right at five. I ran down the stairs and met him at the main door and we walked out to his car. It wasn't an old model pick up but it was nice.

We went out to dinner somewhere nice but not too nice and had a lovely meal. We talked pretty much the whole time about just about everything. He even told me about his time with the War Angels MC getting clean and sober and working on staying that way.

I had known a little about Lachlan's addiction to heroin because Needles helped with that side of the War Angels rehab center but I didn't know what Lachlan had gone through to get to being an addict or how he'd gotten clean.

He didn't tell me his story, or at least no details, only saying some bad shit happened and he couldn't handle it and the heroin took the pain away.

Lachlan didn't ask about Lix or about my being attacked or about the tattoo parlor. He stayed on safe topics like meeting my sister after seventeen years apart, or whether or not I planned on going back to school.

We talked about some of the people who came into my dad's office to have their teeth fixed and laughed at the funnier stories.

When we were finished eating Lachlan paid for our meal and we walked across the parking lot to the movie theater. Just walking inside made me think of Lix but I pushed those feelings away and pasted a smile on my face.

Lix

Was it wrong that I was following Ashlyn on her date? Probably, but I didn't care. I was done being an idiot, I was done being stupid. I needed her back. I didn't care what I had to do to get her back either, she was mine and I had to have her.

I felt like a creep following her, watching her laugh with Lachlan. I had liked Lachlan before this; he was a cool guy who had some serious shadows in his past. Now though if he didn't stop touching Ash I was going to rip his chest open and pull his heart out and feed it to him.

Yeah, I wasn't but I would probably hit him once or twice. Like I said, I liked the guy I just didn't want him anywhere near Ash.

I had been a fool for the last two months. I had been stupid and blind to what I really needed. I'm sounding so selfish, even to my own ears but I had to do something to fix it.

I just wished I wasn't too late. I actually prayed that Ashlyn would take me back and let me love her again.

Over the last month I had talked to my doctor and he thought I was a very good candidate for a cochlear implant. I went and saw the specialist in Vancouver and she scheduled me for the surgery right there.

I was shocked that it could be that easy, it shouldn't be that easy. It was leaving her office that I realized I didn't want to do this without Ashlyn.

Not because I needed her strength, but because she was the first to suggest it and I wanted her to be a part of it coming to fruition. And really, I wanted her voice to be the first I heard.

I could mostly remember what my parents and my sisters sounded like but I had never heard Ashlyn's voice and I knew it would be as beautiful as she was. I could almost imagine the sound of the music her words made as they passed her lips.

Damn I was a fucking stupid idiot. I had finally come to my senses but I might actually be too late.

CHAPTER 15

Ashlyn

Lachlan had been a perfect gentleman, but I got the impression he was interested in someone else. That was ok, I didn't think I would ever be over Lix.

Unfortunately Lix didn't want me anymore. So, I had gone for dinner with Lachlan and had a really great time. Then we got to the theater and watched a movie that reminded me of Lix and had a great time anyway.

We sat in the theater and Lachlan held my hand and it was nice. I really had a great time with him but he wasn't Lix. I knew Lachlan would be a really great friend though.

Now we were sitting in Lachlan's car outside my apartment talking and laughing.

"We're friends aren't we?" Lachlan said suddenly.

"That's not a question is it?" I asked, tipping my head to the side.

"No, not a question," He replied thoughtfully. "You're not over Lix and I am interested in someone else."

"Come up for coffee and tell me about her?" I said reaching for the door handle.

"Absolutely," Lachlan smiled and followed me out. I let us in the building and he followed me up the stairs waiting at my door as I unlocked it. Before I could pull my key out Lachlan was being pushed away from me against the wall.

"Lachlan!" I cried in surprise, turning to find him pinned against the wall of the hallway by Lix. "Lix?"

"I was wondering when you were coming out of hiding, asshole." Lachlan laughed in Lix's face. Lix frowned then pushed away from him and stepped towards me.

"What?" I demanded looking between the two men.

"Yeah, he was following us the whole time we were out. Did you enjoy the movie?" Lachlan asked Lix, smirking at his confusion. "Am I talking too fast? Can't read my lips?"

"Lachlan, stop it." I said, mad at both of them. Mad at Lix for the last two months and mad at Lachlan for knowing Lix was following us and not saying anything and mad that he was making fun of Lix now.

"It's ok, I know you're safe with him," Lachlan said holding his hands up in surrender and nodding at Lix, "But be careful, text me in the morning all right?" He said to me and bent to kiss my cheek. Lix growled low in his throat but Lachlan just chuckled, "Good luck."

And then he was gone and I was standing in the hallway with my ex-boyfriend who had just assaulted my date.

"What the hell is the matter you?" I demanded pushing into the apartment, letting the door swing shut. Lix caught it before it could latch and pushed in behind me.

"Please . . ." he said, grabbing my hand.

"Please?" I pulled my hand away from him so I could sign what I was saying so he didn't miss any of it. *How many times did I say please and you ignored me? You don't get to tell me please and expect me to just give in.*

"I'm sorry,"

You're sorry? Really? Where were you when I was in the hospital healing from being beaten? Where were you when I texted you over and over begging you to come and see me at my dad's? I'm sorry, too because it would seem that ship has sailed.

"No," He shook his head hard, "Please don't say that, let me explain, please talk to me."

"No!" I yelled at him, backing away. *You don't want me, remember? You don't get to follow me around on dates and assault the guys who do want me. You need to leave.*

"Ash –"

"No," I said again pointing at the door. "Leave."

"I will for now, but I'll be back." He said turning and walking out, letting the door slam behind him, like he had any right to be angry.

Lix

Ashlyn was angry, and she had every right to be. I didn't blame her but I couldn't leave her. Now that I had seen her and touched her again it was the hardest thing I did walking out of that apartment. That was as far as I could go, though.

I slumped against the wall beside her door and slid down until I was sitting on the floor and took out my cell phone. I pulled up her name and started typing a text message.

**I never stopped loving you. I believed that
I would never be good enough for you.
I still believe you deserve better than me but
I can't give you up. I've been miserable these
last two months. I almost killed Nick a little while**

**ago because he dared to tell me the truth, that
I'm a dick; that I don't deserve you but you wanted
me anyway, I need you.**

I sent it and waited. I didn't get anything back so I started typing again.

**I will never leave you again. I can't live without you;
I thought I could, knowing you were taken care of.
I thought I could step back and let you be happy
without me but when I saw you smiling with Lachlan
I almost lost my mind. I was jealous and I am stupid.**

I hit send again and waited again. I still didn't get anything back but my phone told me she had read the messages.

**I kept every text message you sent me over the last two months.
I read everyone and saved them. I was dying without
you and those messages were the only things that kept me
going.
I found your old notes in my sketchbook and filled the
rest of the pages with your face. I tore them all out and
hung them up around my room.**

I sent that message and the little bubble with the ellipses came up, showing that she was typing something but nothing came through.

I went to the doctor, saw the specialist in Vancouver.

Where are you?

That apparently got her attention. Instead of answering I stood up and knocked on the door. She yanked it open and looked up at me, her eyes wide in shock.

"You went to the specialist?" She asked, forgetting to sign. I nodded then looked away when I caught movement down the hall. One of her neighbours was coming out of their apartment. I smiled then pushed Ash back into her place and closed the door.

"Why?"

"Because you were right," I said simply. "Because I'm a fucking idiot, because if I'd had them sooner I could have kept you from being hurt."

Ashlyn turned away from me and walked to the windows in the living room. Her arms were crossed protectively across her middle and I could see she was shivering. I walked to her and cupped my hands over her shoulders and squeezed. She took a deep shuddering breath and turned to face me.

What happened that night wasn't your fault.

"I know I'm not to blame, but I was still stupid leaving you out on the sidewalk, especially considering what had happened the last time we had been standing there locking the shop door." I said shaking my head.

You can't take responsibility for what Zane did, and I'm ok now. I'm stronger, I can defend myself. I've been taking classes and working out.

"That's great, I'm glad you are able to do that. I'm glad that you aren't hiding, but Ash baby, it never should have happened." She pushed away from me and walked across the room then turned quickly.

Have you heard anything Zane is saying? I shook my head no, Sharpie had tried to tell me some stuff about the trial and what was going on but I didn't want to know. *Zane said he had been stalking Siobhan's friends for weeks. He said he had been watching the shop, waiting. He was the one who threw the brick; he was trying to kill you. Don't you see?* She signed when I shook my head, *if it wasn't that night it would have been another. He was determined to get me and hurt me, you couldn't have stopped him.*

I shook my head again, not ready or willing to hear her defend me when I knew I was to blame for her pain.

"Stop!" she yelled, grabbing the front of my jacket. She shook me hard then pushed away from me. *You stopped the worst of it. He didn't get a chance to rape me because you stopped him. That's all I care about. The rest is nothing.*

I watched her, gazing deep into her eyes, searching for the recrimination, the blame and the hate but there wasn't any there. I reached out and traced the thin scar on her cheek that she didn't even bother to hide.

"I hurt you." I stated plainly.

"Yes," She said but shook her head. "But not that night."

CHAPTER 16

Ashlyn

I had to make him understand. I had to make him see that I wasn't ready to give him up, that I didn't blame him for Zane's actions.

"I should have gotten the implants when you first brought it up, then I would have been able to save you." He said suddenly. Lix had obviously been thinking about this a lot. I just shrugged because that didn't matter.

Did you not understand what I told you? Zane would have found a way. He would have snatched me when you weren't there. The implants wouldn't have helped, they wouldn't have mattered.

I gazed up into his face, searching for the understanding I needed. I could see the love dripping from his eyes as they filled with tears.

You, me we are the only thing that matters. Do you love me?

He nodded as a tear slipped down his cheek and he fell to his knees in front of me. He laid his head against my stomach and wrapped his arms around my waist, hugging me tightly.

I put my hands on his head and ran my fingers through his hair laughing as my own tears splashed into his curls. He looked up at me in question and I wiped the tears from my cheeks then repeated the process on him.

You need a haircut. He shrugged sheepishly then stood in front of me and wrapped me up in his arms again. *Take me to bed, hold me tonight?*

"Yes please," he said and bent to lift me into his arms and carry me to our room.

We didn't make love that night. He stripped me naked and pulled the t-shirt he had been wearing off and over my head, smoothing it over me and covering me. Then he stripped out of his own clothes, leaving on his boxers and pulled back the covers, helping me slide under them and following me into bed.

He turned to me and pulled me into his arms, my back to his front, one arm under my head and around my shoulders and the other around my middle.

"I love you," He whispered in my ear then kissed down my neck, burying his nose in my hair. I tapped the arm around my waist and he lifted his head.

I showed him the sign for I love you and he buried his face in my neck again but I could feel him smile and then we both drifted into the first decent sleep either of us had gotten in the last two months.

The next morning was Saturday. I rolled away from Lix but he reached for me, trying to pull me back. I looked at him and laughed as he cracked open an eye and showed him the sign for 'potty'.

He smiled then and let me go, rolling over onto his back and going back to sleep. When I came back I crawled in beside him and cuddled up into his side, laying my head on his shoulder.

Hours later I woke up again alone in the bed. I sat up and stretched looking around the room. Lix's pants were gone and I could smell coffee from the kitchen. I could also hear voices from the living room but none of them were Lix. I frowned and got up, pulling on sweat pants and slipping into the bathroom to brush my teeth.

When I came out I found my dad right in Lix's face yelling at him while Lix stood and took the abuse. Pixie and Seether were sitting on the couch watching.

"What the hell is going on here?" I demanded angrily.

Lix

I woke up that morning to a flashing beyond my eyelids. I remembered Ash getting up to go to the bathroom then cuddling back in with me. Looking at the clock I saw that it was ten in the morning and then the lights flashed again. Someone was at the door. I looked over at Ash but she just buried her head under the blankets and stayed asleep.

I got up and grabbed my jeans and pulled them on and went to open the door. To say I was surprised by the fist in my face was an understatement. When I recovered enough to see who was at the door I found Ash's dad shoving past me into the apartment. Then Pixie pushed past me after her uncle saying something that I didn't catch and Seether clapped a hand over my shoulder.

"What the fuck is going on?" I demanded, touching my nose with the back of my hand, looking for blood.

Lachlan called Siobhan and told her you were here last night, Siobhan called Pixie and her uncle just happened to be at our house at the time. Seether signed shrugging.

"Fuck," I said turning to walk the rest of the way into the apartment. I couldn't hear James yelling but I could tell that he was, right in Pixie's face where I'm sure she was trying to calm him down. When he saw me come into the room he pointed at me and yelled something. Seether went to sign it for me but I waved him off, "Don't bother, let him yell it'll make him feel better."

So, for the next half an hour or so, while a very pregnant Pixie made coffee and Seether relaxed on the couch I let Ash's dad yell at me. I stood in the middle of the room with my hands on my hips and my head bowed and let the man rant.

I couldn't hear a word he said of course but I could figure out the jist from the few words I read on his lips. I was just about to raise my hands and ask him to calm down so I could explain when everyone's attention suddenly swung to the far end of the room. I looked up to find a very angry Ashlyn standing glaring at everyone.

Dad, what are you doing here? She signed as she spoke.

"Rightfully giving me hell," I replied for him, smiling sheepishly at Ash.

Don't be ridiculous, I'm the only one allowed to give you hell about anything. I was about to say something else in defense of James when Ash's attention shot to Pixie on the couch, and then everything went nuts and Seether was losing his mind.

"What's going on?" I demanded so confused.

Pixie's water broke. Ash signed then ran to put on shoes.

"Ash, I need my shirt." I told her as she was putting her coat on.

"Shit!" She dropped her coat on the floor and rushed into the bedroom then came back a second later and tossed me my shirt.

After that there was a lot of rushing and once we got to the hospital there was a lot of waiting. I texted Lo to put the word out that Pixie was in labour and within the hour most of the MC was at the hospital in the waiting room with us.

Hours later I was sitting in a very uncomfortable chair with my head back and my eyes closed. Ashlyn was on my lap and snuggled against my chest and then suddenly she was gone.

I opened my eyes to find her standing in front of Seether a huge beaming smile on both their faces. Then she was hopping up and down and throwing herself into his arms and hugging him tight.

I sat and waited because I knew someone would tell me what was going on and I was right. Ash turned around and threw herself back into my arms and I felt her hot tears soaking my shirt.

"What's the matter?" I demanded pulling away to look at her. I didn't understand the tears at first because her smile was so big I thought her cheeks might split but then she started signing so fast I was having trouble keeping up.

It's a girl!! Pixie had a girl! Her name is Aubrey Claire! I'm an auntie!!

Ashlyn was so excited her happiness was contagious and I thought my heart would burst with it. I grabbed her and turned her in a circle, holding her tight to my chest.

"Congratulations Auntie," I laughed in her ear then turned to Seether and held a hand out to him, shaking his as I congratulated him as well.

CHAPTER 17

Lix

Pixie had gone home with little Aubrey after a couple of days and her and Seether were settling in with their baby. Ash stopped by their place every couple of days to get her baby fix as she called it and make sure Pixie didn't need anything.

Ashlyn and I were close to being back to where we had been before but there was something missing. Ash hadn't been back to the tattoo parlor, either to work or visit and I felt that maybe she was still dealing with that trauma. I suggested she talk to Brooke about it and she nodded but didn't say anything else about it.

We also hadn't made love. We slept in each other's arms every night and every morning we woke up together and got ready for the day together but we never crossed that line. There was a lot of kissing and even some heavy petting but we seemed to have an unspoken agreement that we were starting over in everything and that would have to wait, at least I thought it was an agreement.

I had noticed quite a few changes in Ash's body and in her routine. She no longer sat in the window to draw when she was troubled, now she spent most of her time in the apartment building's gym working out or sparring with her trainer. She would come home from her dad's office after a difficult day and instantly change into workout clothes and head down to the gym.

More often than not if I was home I joined her and even sparred with her a few times. She was a beast in the gym and I was glad I was in good shape and worked out regularly myself or I would never have been able to keep up with her.

Now when we cuddled I found my hands drifting over hard muscle where before there were soft feminine curves. Ashlyn's shoulders were broader and thicker with muscle and her soft flat belly had been replaced with rigid abs. I loved her body, before and now but I missed her softness, her body's obvious differences from mine.

She was also more pensive than before, where before she was attacked she was always quick to jump into a new project now she stepped back and thought long and hard about joining in something if she didn't know all the players. She was nervous and often jumpy, too. If I walked up to her while she was lost in thought and she didn't hear me coming she would jump and her pulse would race.

It was those times especially that I would mention talking to Brooke, or if not Brooke then the therapist that Pixie saw after she was attacked. Ashlyn would nod her head in agreement and then shrug her shoulders and go back to whatever it was she was doing. Going to the gym hadn't just replaced her art during times when she was troubled, either. It seemed that Ashlyn had stopped drawing all together.

I often had my own art supplies spread around the apartment and if she looked at them at all it was with disdain. It was like she despised those things. Once I found her sitting on our couch with my sketch pad open in her lap and she was flipping through the pictures with tears streaming down her cheeks.

When I looked closer it was the sketchbook I had drawn her in so many times when we were apart. When I sat beside her on the couch wanting to comfort her she dumped the book in my lap and rushed out of the room and down to the gym to work out. When she came back a few hours later she went straight to the shower and then climbed into bed without saying a word to me.

I was finally beyond what I could handle and Ash wouldn't talk to me about how she was feeling. I didn't know what to do anymore and talking to her dad wasn't an option anymore.

I tried talking to my mom but she didn't know Ashlyn well enough to be able to give me any advice beyond loving her. I could do that, I was doing that but there was still something I was missing. I finally made up my mind and went knocking on Lachlan's door.

Ashlyn

I was lost. Oh, not physically, I knew exactly where I was in the physical sense sitting cross legged in the middle of our bed, but I was lost. I couldn't get my brain to work right. Lix had been asking me to see a therapist to help deal with the trauma from the attack but I just couldn't make myself take that step.

I knew he was frustrated with me and my inability to talk to him, or even talk at all. I didn't realize it because he couldn't hear anyway but I had almost completely stopped talking. I hadn't told him but I had almost completely stopped going to see Pixie and the baby.

If she had told him he hadn't said anything. I still went to work but didn't speak to anyone there either. Lix wanted me to talk to Brooke or another therapist but I couldn't even force myself to say no, or yes or maybe or . . . anything.

I was lost in my own head. My brain had so many thoughts and things running around in it but I couldn't get them out. Even at night my thoughts ran constantly, to the point that I couldn't think.

Lix didn't realize it but the reason I worked out so much was because I couldn't think of another way to exhaust myself enough to actually sleep. I wanted to draw but when I sat down with a sketchbook and a pencil nothing happened. I could stare at a blank page for hours and nothing would happen. The pencil would touch the page and stay there for hours.

I was still sitting in that spot when Lix came home and found me sitting on the bed. I was staring off into space and didn't realize he'd walked in until he kneeled on the floor right in my line of sight. I jumped when he appeared even though I was sure he'd been calling my name but I was far too lost in my thoughts to have heard him.

"Baby," he said smiling slightly. I hated that smile. That was the 'I know something is wrong' smile and 'I want to fix it for you', only I didn't think this could be fixed. "I brought someone to talk to you, think you're up for a visitor?"

I don't know if I did anything more than blink at Lix but he smiled again and stood, kissing my forehead. Then someone else was in the room and Lix was telling them he was going to be in the living room if they needed anything.

"Ash," Lachlan breathed sitting beside me on the bed. I turned to look at him, confused. "What's going on Ash?"

I didn't have an answer for him because I didn't know. I wanted to tell him but I didn't know how.

"You're not talking anymore Ash?" I blinked.

"You're worrying a lot of people, Ash." He stated and I blinked again then sighed. "Tell you what, blink once for yes and twice for no." I blinked.

"Good, are you scared?" I blinked.

"Are you confused?" I blinked.

"Are you angry?" I blinked . . . twice.

"Good, you're stuck in your head." Blink.

"You need to see a therapist." Blink . . . and shrug.

"Lix is really worried about you." Lachlan said touching my hand. "He's so worried about you that he actually came to me because he knew you and I are friends. We're friends aren't we, Ash?" Blink.

"Good, then you need to see a therapist. Lix is scared; he doesn't know how to help you." Lachlan sighed, "If we set up an appointment with the therapist that Pixie saw will you see her?" Blink.

"Ok, I'm going to go and talk to Lix. Have you slept recently?" Two blinks. "Are you having nightmares?" I frowned at that because I couldn't really say I was having bad dreams, they were dark but there was nothing specifically that I could pull out and say was bad other than a feeling. "I'm going to take that as a yes even without the blink. Have you tried taking anything to help you sleep?"

That time I shook my head no.

"Would you consider taking a Nytol or Gravol to help you sleep?" This time I shrugged and he nodded then kissed the side of my head and left the room. A few minutes later Lix came in with a pink pill and a glass of water.

"Just Gravol," He said, putting it in my hand. I took the pill and drank the water and lay down in the bed, letting him cover me up and then he was gone.

Within minutes, partially because of the pill and I'm sure partially because of my level of exhaustion I was asleep.

CHAPTER 18

Lix

I walked out of our room after tucking Ash into bed to find Lachlan sitting on the couch in the living room. He looked up when he heard me close the door and gave me a grim smile.

"It's bad, right?" I asked him, slumping into the armchair. He nodded and started talking but I stopped him. "I can't hear you."

A look of 'oh shit' crossed his face and then he looked chagrined.

"You don't know sign?" He shook his head no so I got up and grabbed some paper and a pen.

Yes it's bad, he wrote, **at least in my very unprofessional opinion. I've only taken a few psych classes but I wouldn't be surprised if she was suffering from PTSD.**

"Fuck, what do I do now?" I asked him, rubbing a hand over my face.

Get her help, even if that means forcing her to get it. She's not well and she's hiding. She said she hasn't been having nightmares?

"I don't know about that," I said shaking my head. "When she sleeps she's restless but I don't think she's ever cried out. I've tried to stay up and watch her sleep but I inevitably fall asleep and when I wake up she's gone."

That's ok, you can't stay up like that, either. She's not drawing? I shook my head no. **I wonder if she'd write?**

"Like stories?"

Or a journal.

"I don't know but I suppose it's worth a try. In the beginning she and I used to communicate a lot like this with notes until she learned sign. She might write in a journal."

I didn't know what else to do but Ash had agreed to see a therapist and I was getting that number from Pixie now, before I did anything else.

Ashlyn

"NOOOOO!" I was sitting up in bed and I was sweating. Lix was sitting in front of me, his hands on my shoulders, shaking me slightly.

"Wake up Ash!" he yelled in my face, his hot breath on my face. He was scowling but I could see the fear in his eyes.

"What happened?" I asked panting.

"I don't know," Lix said, shaking his head and sitting back away from me like he was exhausted, like he had just run the longest, hardest race of his life. "I don't know what happened, one minute you were asleep, and then you were having a dream and you started thrashing and then you were sitting up and your mouth was wide open and I could just imagine you were screaming. Fuck Ash, I was so scared. You weren't coming out of it."

"Sorry," I whispered, not knowing what else to say.

"Fuck," he breathed, grabbing fistfuls of his hair and falling back, his head laying at the foot of the bed and I could see him breathing hard. "This has to stop, you don't say or sign a word for a week, all you do is work out and then the first time any sound comes out of your mouth it's screaming."

Lix sat up again and stared deep into my eyes. "I called Pixie's therapist. She's coming to see you tomorrow."

"No, I –" I was shaking my head.

"No Ash!" he yelled again, cutting me off. "You can't live like this anymore, I can't live like this. I'm going to Vancouver in five days for surgery for cochlear implants and you're going with me and I don't want the first time I hear your voice to be you screaming in terror."

"I'm sorry," I cried, feeling my eyes fill with tears that I couldn't control anymore. I took a deep breath and let the tears spill down my cheeks and then I was sobbing and I couldn't catch my breath as I stared at him. "I'm so sorry; I don't know what to do. I can't find me."

"Oh Ash," he breathed, sitting forward and pulling me into his lap. We sat like that for a long time, me in his lap crying and him with his arms wrapped around me murmuring in my ear how much he loved me and cared and was sorry.

"He raped me," I finally said when the tears finally dried up enough that I could speak.

"What?" Lix demanded pulling away from me.

"He raped me," I repeated, locking my gaze with his.

"No, he didn't." Lix stated, shaking his head. "I stopped him before I could rape you, he didn't get that far."

"That's not what my head tells me." I whispered then tucked my head under his chin and let him take all my weight. I don't know how long we sat that way, but eventually I felt him turning me and laying me down on the bed and curling himself around my back, pulling the covers over us.

The next morning I woke up alone, disoriented and cranky. I rubbed the sleep out of my eyes and sat up. I turned when the door opened and saw Lix standing there.

"I was just coming to wake you up, the therapist will be here in about an hour, I thought you'd want to get ready before she got her." He said smiling slightly.

I nodded and got out of bed, moving slowly to the bathroom. I probably spent way too much time in the shower but I didn't care, it felt good. For the first time in months something felt good.

When I finally came out of the bathroom Lix was there with Pixie's therapist. I remembered her from one session Pixie asked me to be a part of during her healing process. I found it informative but heartbreaking. What were the odds that I was now seeing the same therapist for a similar reason?

Margaret stepped forward holding her hands out to me and smiling.

"How are you Ashlyn?" she asked when I let her take my hands in hers.

"Ok, I guess." I replied shrugging.

"I'm glad to hear you're talking again, Felix said you hadn't been speaking." Margaret never took her eyes from mine.

"Oh," I wasn't sure how to respond to that. "Lix can't hear, he wouldn't know I wasn't actually speaking."

Margaret chuckled at that, "Ok then, he said you stopped communicating, is that better?"

I nodded and shrugged, not sure if that was better or it just was.

"So, Felix said he'd leave if you want him to, or he can stay, but it's completely up to you." Margaret said glancing at Lix.

"If you want I will completely leave the apartment, or I'll just go in our room, or I'll sit here on the armchair. I can't hear what you say and I promise if you want me to stay I won't read your lips." Lix said, seeming to take his cue from Margaret.

"Stay," I whispered glancing at him.

"Stay?" He repeated and I nodded. Margaret led me to the couch and sat down and Lix sat in the armchair with his sketchpad. The whole thing was somehow comforting, Margaret's soft voice, her warm hands holding mine, the sound of Lix's pencil on the page as he drew.

Is this what I had been missing? I couldn't say I felt better exactly but the gray pushing at my vision was slightly brighter.

"Felix said you were dreaming the man who attacked you raped you when he actually didn't." Margaret said suddenly, "Why do you think that is?"

I shook my head confused, "I don't know. He said he was going to. He was pulling at my pants and his belt buckle; he was on top of me…"

"Have you and Felix been intimate since that night?"

"We've slept together, we always sleep together."

"Good, but I mean have you had intercourse?"

I shook my head again scowling, "No, he doesn't want to."

"Oh?" Margaret was surprised, honestly so was I. "Did he say that?"

"No, he just hasn't made that move."

"Have you asked him about it?" I shook my head no again and looked at my hands. "Do you want to? He's right here."

"That's embarrassing," I whispered, not able to look up at Margaret.

"Write it down." Margaret said, shrugging. "Then if you want to give him the note you can and if you decide not to, you don't have to."

I reached for the sketchpad on the coffee table and listened as Lix's pencil stopped moving and he watched me then he went back to drawing. I wrote the note, the one question that had weighed so heavy on my mind. The whole two months we had been apart I had thought he didn't want me and now we were back together and he wasn't making love to me.

Did I need to know why?

Did I need to know why right now?

Was I ready to hear the answer?

I think I had to know the answer.

I tore the page from the sketchbook and placed it on Lix's lap under his line of sight. His pencil lifted and he looked up at me, tears in his eyes.

"This is my fault."

CHAPTER 19

Lix

When Ash had reached for that sketchpad I had such hope that she would start drawing. I watched until she picked up a pen and not a pencil before I went back to my own art.

Ash never drew with a pen, doodled maybe but she never doodled in a sketchbook. Maybe I was reading too much into this, maybe for now she would get over her ideas and doodle in a sketchbook with a pen and forget about the purity of the art.

I went back to my own drawing, not ignoring Ash and Margaret but not really paying super close attention to them either. It wasn't until that scrap of paper landed on my drawing and I read what Ash had written that I started to break down. I watched a tear fall from my eye and stain the page, making the ink run.

Why won't you make love to me? She had written in her pretty script that I loved so much. I had done this to her, I had thought we were on the same page but we had stopped communicating and really talking to each other. Then I read the second sentence and I couldn't stop the sob in my chest from escaping. Is it because of what he did?

"This is my fault." I said looking up at her letting the tears flow down my cheeks. "I did this to you; my God I'm so sorry."

I launched myself out of the chair and across the coffee table to her, wrapping her in my arms and crying into her hair. I don't remember what I said, but I'm sure it sounded ridiculous and probably too loud.

I know I said 'I'm sorry' over and over again, with 'I love you's peppered in. I couldn't stop and finally I pulled back and cupped her face in my hands, her still damp hair wrapped around my fingers.

"I love you so much, I am so sorry I didn't talk to you about this." I sniffed and blew out a breath. "I want to make love to you so much. I thought I was giving you time, I thought we were starting over with everything. I thought we were waiting for I don't know what."

Ashlyn frowned at me and shook her head as much as she could with me holding her still.

"I didn't want to pressure into anything. I knew I had hurt you those two months and I didn't want you to think I came back to you for sex. I came back to you for you because I can't live without you, because I tried and I just don't want to."

"Lix," she said, reaching up to cup my cheeks and kiss me, then she pulled back just slightly to mouth the words 'I love you' against my lips. Then she sat back, taking her hands back and pulling out of my grasp.

I need this. She signed motioning to Margaret. I nodded, knowing she meant that she needed the therapy sessions with Margaret. *But I need you, too.*

"Well," Margaret said, Ash blew out a breath and wiped the tears from her cheeks then signed for Margaret so I would know what she was saying. "It would seem that we've had a breakthrough. I want to keep seeing you, though Ashlyn. You're suffering from PTSD."

Ash nodded and shrugged, *I figured.*

"When are you going for your implants?" Margaret asked me.

"Five days." I replied, not taking my eyes off of Ash.

"Then Ashlyn, I would like to see you at least one more time before you go to Vancouver. After that I would like to see you at least once a week but for sure more if you feel it's necessary." Margaret said and Ash finally yanked her gaze from mine to Margaret's. "I think it's necessary but I'm not going to pressure you. You can call me any time if you feel you want to come in to talk no matter what time of the day or night."

"Ok," Ash said nodding then returned her gaze to mine.

"Well, I think that's my cue to leave." Margaret said laughing as she stood. I stood with her and walked her to the door.

"Thank you so much." I said quietly, my voice thick with emotion.

"You should come in also." Margaret said slowly so I could read her lips then she patted my chest and walked out the door. When I turned Ash was standing in the middle of the room, playing with the hem of her shirt.

"Do you want me to run you a bath?" I asked, not moving any closer.

Will you join me?

"If you want me to, yes I would love to." I whispered and she nodded smiling slightly.

Ashlyn

Lix still didn't make love to me that night but that was ok, after such an emotional couple of days it wouldn't have been right. We enjoyed our bath; we petted and kissed and enjoyed each other but didn't cross that line.

I saw Margaret again the afternoon before we left for Vancouver and had a very good talk with her. I don't know why it had taken me so long to seek out therapy but I really wish I had done it sooner.

That morning Sharpie had stopped by the apartment to tell us about Dean Zane's trial. Things were progressing, he said but Zane was trying to slow things down with motions and briefs and anything he could think of. Sharpie wasn't that kind of attorney so he couldn't help us with the trial; he could only give us advice. That was fine, that's really what I needed.

Lix and I left for Vancouver early in the morning. We decided that we should have a mini holiday in the city before he had to be at the hospital for his surgery. We stayed at a big hotel in a room with a king size bed and a Jacuzzi tub and a fireplace that we made love in front of. It was the perfect night.

Lix made love to me slow and gentle and seemed to be savoring every inch of me. I orgasmed twice before he raised himself over me and thrust deep inside, kissing my lips as though he would never get enough. It felt like a whole new beginning, like we were really starting everything fresh from this night.

The next morning we got up bright and early and made our way to the hospital and checked in. We knew this would not be an easy fix. Lix had talked to the surgeon before and he learned everything he needed to know. I had been reading the information he had gotten when my life went to hell and my PTSD invaded. As he drove the three hours to the city I reread everything I had looked at before and read as much as I could have what would happen after the surgery.

Lix would go into the OR and get local anesthetic behind his ears. The surgeon would make an incision behind his ears and move the mastoid bone and identify the facial nerves. He would then insert the implant and attach it to Lix's skull then close everything up and Lix would be taken to recovery where I was waiting for him.

That's where I was sitting when a noise from the doors of the waiting room alerted me to the presence of more people. When I looked up I saw Pixie and Seether with baby Aubrey as well as Lo, Alana and their kids, Axle, Brooke and Imogen, Hammer, Kat and their triplets, Needles and Siobhan and Nick. I was in shock to say the least; that all these people would come out to support Lix. Before I could say anything the door opened again and my dad walked in.

"What -?"

"You didn't think we would miss this did you, Ash?" Kat asked, smiling at me. "All these guys were there when Sam had his surgery, what makes you think they wouldn't be here for Lix's?"

I smiled at everyone and felt my eyes well with tears and Pixie sat beside me and wrapped me in her arms.

"How are you?" She asked quietly.

"I'm ok," I replied smiling at her, "Better than I was. I'm sorry I cut you out."

"Don't be, you suffered a trauma and you were lost. I'm glad that Margaret is helping you. She's amazing."

"Do you still see her?" I asked, turning to face my sister.

"Once a month or so, every so often Aiden will look at me and tell me to call her. Sometimes it's more than once a month sometimes it's every six weeks. Aiden reads me so well; he always knows when I need more than he can give me." I nodded, understanding exactly what she meant.

It wasn't that Aiden loved her any less or that he wouldn't do anything for her, it was just that he wasn't trained to help her through the remnants of her trauma.

It wasn't long after that the nurse came in to tell us that Lix was in recovery and I could go in and see him.

She said he was probably sore and tired from the anesthesia and we should take it easy with visiting and he would be able to leave in a couple of hours.

CHAPTER 20

Lix

After the surgery a nurse wheeled my bed to a recovery room that was full of other patients also recovering from different procedures, each section divided by a privacy curtain.

I immediately fell asleep even though I knew that Ash would be coming in. I wanted to see her but after the last couple of days and not sleeping much last night I was exhausted and the anesthesia was still running through my system.

I opened my eyes at one point when I felt Ashlyn kiss my forehead and caught a flash of movement around me but I ignored it and let her soothe me back to sleep, brushing my hair gently off my forehead.

The next time I opened my eyes only Saint was in the room, or the curtains. I lifted my head and sat up slightly, wincing at the slight pain behind my ears.

"Where's Ash?" I could tell by the feel of my throat that my voice was raspy so not very loud.

Everyone went down to the cafeteria to get some coffee. Saint signed, not bothering to speak as he did.

"Everyone?"

Everyone. He signed smiling. *You should see the nurses, freaking out about most of an MC being in the waiting room.*

I chuckled at that, wishing I had seen it. I rubbed a hand over my eyes grimacing at how my stitches pulled then looked at Saint when he tapped my hand.

How are things? At my confused look he rolled his eyes. *With Ash? With the implants?*

"Oh, yeah. Everything is good so far." I replied, taking a deep breath. "Ash is seeing a counsellor and I got the implants and pulled my head outta my ass." Saint smirked at that and shook his head.

Glad to hear it. He signed nodding. *We're good?*

"Fuck man, you think I'm mad at you because you told me the truth? That I was being stupid and needed to pull my head outta my ass?" Saint shrugged and nodded. "No man, I'm not mad, at least not at you. Me, yeah I'm mad at me for wasting a fucking month with the best thing in my world."

Your family isn't here?

"I didn't tell them," I replied, shaking my head slightly. "I wanted to surprise them. Poor Ash, I made her promise not to say anything either. She's not very good at keeping secrets and she hates having to do it."

That's kind of mean, man. Saint snickered.

"Why are you here but Casey isn't?" I asked, frowning. "I thought you guys were a thing?"

Saint sighed and shrugged unhappily, *She broke up with me, won't even talk to me. I asked Siobhan and she said Casey is completely broken up but she feels she did what was best for me.*

"Did she tell you why?"

She can't have kids, she thinks I want a house full of my own and she can't give them to me so I should be free to find someone who can give them to me. Saint was obviously completely ripped apart by that.

I could tell, seeing him with Casey that he was falling in love with her and it looked like the feeling was mutual.

Saint did love kids, he volunteered as a big brother and was always at one after school program or another, helping out with the kids most at risk of getting involved in shit that would get them in trouble, or killed.

"Shit man, that sucks," I said shaking my head. He just shrugged and sighed. "That why you were so mad that day in the kitchen?" He nodded sheepishly and I nodded back in understanding. "I get it, we're good. If it wasn't for you I wouldn't have Ash back, I wouldn't have taken the steps I did to be in this bed right now. I really hope you can make Casey see the light."

Saint shrugged and shook his head, *I think it's a lost cause* he signed and then turned his head to the door just as Ash and the others came in the door.

Oh hey, you're awake! Are you ready to get out of here? I nodded with an expression I hoped said oh hell ya and she seemed to laugh. *I'll get the nurse.*

Before she could go Saint took her hand and pulled her into the chair he had been sitting in and said something to her then left the room.

The nurse came in and then the surgeon, kicking everyone else out of the room, they checked me out, declared me good enough to leave and kicked me out, too.

We all decided since half the MC was here and it was spring we would stay another night in the city. Vancouver was a beautiful city and there was so much to do and it was a rare sunny afternoon.

The sky had not a single cloud and was blue and bright. The sun was warm and we were able to walk around town with just sweaters on. Amazing how the weather changed so drastically after a three hour drive.

Ashlyn

Lo and Alana got everyone checked into the same hotel as us then we all met in the lobby to decide what we would do for the afternoon. It was late February, almost March and there were so many options available.

We decided to go to Stanley Park and walk around the Sea Wall, stroll on the beach, then ride the train and walk through the Aquarium.

We didn't want to do anything too strenuous that would cause Lix discomfort and walks through the most beautiful park in the world were just the perfect thing.

By the time we got back to the hotel Lix was exhausted, but so were the kids so at least their parents were able to get some sleep. I think Lo had the most fun, spoiling his step-sons even though Alana told him not to but he didn't listen.

He had adopted her youngest son, Drew just after they were married and even though the boy was almost eight, Lo carried him around on his shoulders almost the whole day.

Everyone had so much fun and I was so glad they had descended on us at the hospital. Lix was a part of this crazy family and because of him and Pixie so was I.

Growing up my family hadn't been large, with just dad, mom and I and then my step-mom but our house had always been full of love.

Even when my mom got angry that she couldn't have kids of her own and when she died I still knew she loved me. This big family though was different. There was always laughter and love and I felt so blessed to be a part of it.

We had to wait five weeks before Lix's incisions and implants had healed enough and the swelling had gone down for him to actually receive the external parts of his implant.

It included a microphone, speech processor and a transmitter and Lix and I needed to learn how to use it and take care of it.

It wasn't a tiny mostly invisible thing that was placed in the ear like most hearing aids. It was a bigger piece that hooked onto the ear and had a coil that magnetically attached behind Lix's ear.

There was so much training Lix had to go through to relearn how to hear. The implant wouldn't make his hearing perfect, but he would be able to hear and that was all he cared about.

We even got him a cell phone that had specific technology for his implant so he would no longer have to only text.

He still hadn't told his parents about the implant but he had a special surprise for them once it was done.

Luckily there was an audiologist in Kamloops who could fit the external parts of the implant and do the therapy he needed to learn how to use it. Once again half of the MC was sitting in a waiting room, waiting.

Lix had gone into have the external parts fitted and we were waiting until we could be let into the room to actually talk to him. We were all so nervous that this wouldn't work so when the doctor came out of the office to tell us Lix was ready I jumped out of my chair.

"Don't worry," the doctor said, "All the tests so far have shown that the implant is working perfectly. Felix still hasn't heard anyone's voice though. He made me promise not to actually speak to him until he could talk to Ashlyn first. He said yours was the first voice he wanted to hear."

CHAPTER 21

Lix

I was sitting on the exam table in that room waiting for the greatest day of my life. I was getting nervous, though waiting for the doctor to bring Ash and the others in. No one knew what I had planned but I wanted the first voice I heard to be Ash's and I wanted the first word I heard from her to be yes.

When the door opened and the doctor ushered her in I stood from the table and held out my hand to her. She came quickly and opened her mouth to say something but I stopped her.

"Ash, baby," I whispered, knowing I was whispering. "I wanted yours to be the first voice I heard, but there's only one thing I want to know, will you marry me?"

"Yes!" she didn't even hesitate for a second, "Yes I will marry you!"

I laughed and threw my head back. "I heard you! I can hear you!" I wrapped my arms around her waist, picking her up and spun her in a circle.

We celebrated that night and I heard every sound and whisper and song that was playing around me. It was absolutely amazing.

The next morning I texted my sisters and told them they all had to be at our parent's house by supper time, that Ash and I had news for them. They all texted back and wanted to know what it was but I ignored each and every message. I knew they would be too curious not to show up.

Ash and I spent a lazy morning in bed, and I reveled in every sound she made as I licked and kissed and worshiped her body. Sex with Ashlyn was always amazing, but now that I could hear her, every gasp and moan and whimper, making love with her was cataclysmic.

After her second orgasm I couldn't wait anymore. I rolled onto my back and pulled her to straddle me. She stared down at me in shock with her hands on my chest, breathing hard, her eyes wide.

"Ride me baby . . . fuck I want to see you come apart at the same time as I hear it." She smiled and leaned down and kissed me deeply, sliding her tongue against mine then sat up and gripped my aching cock in her hand.

She held it as she slid my dick into her hot wet sheath, throwing her head back on a groan as I filled her. Before she could slide down all the way I thrust up into her, gripping her hips in my hands and kneading her with my fingers. She gasped and dipped her chin to her chest, closing her eyes.

Slowly I positioned my thumb over her clit and rubbed it in circles, making her rise and fall over me faster. I pulled my knees up for her to rest against as she moved and gave me better access to her core, her ass rubbing on my thighs with every move she made. The diamond on her finger that I had given her yesterday sparkled in the sun from the windows and I knew I had everything I ever wanted.

"Baby, play with your tits, pinch your nipples . . . make yourself come around me Ash," I rasped, watching her and hearing her and just about to come myself from the sensations.

Her hands left my wrists where she had been gripping me and did as I asked, arching her back off my legs, her inner muscles gripping my cock in a strangling grip. She cried out, keening as her release gushed hot and wet around my dick and I couldn't hold back anymore.

I gripped her hips hard and pumped into her furiously until I felt my balls inch up and the tingle in my lower back and I emptied my cum deep inside her. As we both came down from heaven I levered up and wrapped my arms around her, holding her tight against my chest.

"I love you so much," I whispered in her ear, kissing her hair and cupping the back of her head, tucking her under my chin.

"I love you, too." She panted, kissing my chest, my throat and across my jaw to my lips. "Let's shower; we have to get to Kelowna."

We did shower, taking our time and making love again under the hot spray. Ash was still working out quite a bit but not as much as before. She still had a lot of muscle tone but she was also softening up in the places I missed her femininity.

The drive to Kelowna was slow with a lot of stops at fruit stands and little mom and pop spots along the way. It was still early April so there wasn't a lot at the fruit stands but spring in the Okanagan was a beautiful time.

When we got to my parent's house we climbed out of my truck and stood on the sidewalk. There were enough cars parked along the street that I knew my sisters and brothers-in-law were all inside. I pulled out my phone and dialed my mom's cell phone.

"Hello?"

"Hi mom," I answered smiling, watching the house.

"Who is this?" she demanded, confused.

"It's Felix, mom," I laughed.

"Felix? How are you calling me?"

"Look out the window mom," I said then hung up the phone. I saw her peek through the lace curtains she loved so much and watched her face light up then she was out the front door and running down the path to the sidewalk.

"What is going on Felix?" She demanded when she got to me, throwing her arms around my shoulders. "You text your sisters to be here for supper and don't tell me or your dad anything and then you call me?"

I knew she thought I couldn't hear her so I laughed then grasped her shoulders and pushed her back gently.

"Mom, I texted everyone to be here because Ash and I have a couple of surprises for you," I said looking into her eyes.

"You can hear me . . . " she gasped, her hands flying to her mouth as tears filled her eyes.

"Yeah mom," I replied smiling, my own eyes feeling hot, "I can hear you."

The rest of the evening was full of excitement and talking. Often my family forgot I could hear them and would sign what they were saying. We celebrated again, not just my hearing but also Ashlyn and I getting engaged.

She was only turning nineteen this summer so we decided to wait until she was twenty. I thought she would be upset that I wanted that but she just shrugged and smiled.

After supper was over we were all sitting in the living room, the TV turned off and couples sitting together in chairs and on the couch.

"So um," Ash suddenly cleared her throat in a lull in the conversation. "I have another announcement to make."

We all looked at her and she blushed, obviously nervous. She moved to get off my lap and stand in front of everyone and I helped her, just as curious as everyone else.

"Um, well, we're not just engaged."

"What do you mean babe?" I asked frowning, "Did we get married and I didn't know about it?" Everyone laughed, even Ash but she sobered quickly.

"No, we're not married, yet. We are pregnant." She replied, watching my face and biting her lower lip. I blinked at her in shock, then knelt on the floor in front of her and kissed her stomach.

"My baby is in here?" I asked, looking up at her. She nodded, still biting that lip as tears slid down her cheeks. I stood and wrapped my arms around her, whispering in her ear, "Thank you. You've given me everything, you are my everything."

"You are my everything," she said, letting me kiss her deeply as my family cheered around us.

Printed in Great Britain
by Amazon

86191939R00078